Praise for *The Riddled Stone* Series

"A captivating fantasy story with a well-thought-out plot … the excitement, adventure, and suspense will easily keep the reader's attention."

—Wayne S. Walker, *Home School Book Review*

"Enjoyable … a quick and easy read, and a good story."

—Katie Grace, online reader review

"Intriguing … There are many new languages unearthed, magic uncovered, and creatures unleashed … I enjoyed the book and I am absolutely amazed at how such a young author can write so well. I definitely see her going far in her writing career, and I can't wait to see what stories she publishes next."

—Tia, *Homeschool Literature.com*

… Even as Arnold shouted and signaled Rich with a nudge of his heel, he was slipping his shield from his back and over his arm. He could see lumps on the ground—almost a dozen bodies—and one man fleeing the scene. A handful of ragged-looking men watched him go. The biggest of the bandits stood several feet closer than the main group, leaning over a fallen body.

Arnold tilted his arm up to keep the shield from falling as one by one he bent the prosthetic fingers into place. The distance between him and the big man narrowed. He had two fingers left to go and no time.

Without drawing his sword, he bumped his knee against Rich's side. The horse veered to the right, and Arnold swung his shield at the man. The bandit jumped backwards, but not fast enough. The bottom of the shield clipped his chin, throwing him to the ground.

Arnold sat back, and Rich ground to a halt. As he drew his blade, a quick squeeze of his foot made the horse pivot to face the other bandits. They were leaping aside to avoid Chris, who had cantered down the slope at Arnold's heels.

"Behind you!" shouted Terrin from atop the hill.

Arnold spun Rich to see that the first man had clambered back to his feet, sword in hand. He charged, ready to skewer the man, but the bandit slipped out of reach. Rich pivoted to face the man again and reared, his hooves thrashing.

The bandit leaped back, across the body he'd been standing over. A woman, or a youth? Arnold couldn't tell for sure. The man pointed his sword at the still form. "Make one move, and I end this one's life."

Arnold lowered his sword …

BETRAYED

THE RIDDLED STONE
BOOK THREE

Teresa Gaskins

Tabletop Academy Press

CONTENTS

Annotated Cast of Characters.. ix

Part One 1

Part Two...65

Part Three..135

About the Author 211

ANNOTATED CAST OF CHARACTERS

The Original Companions

CHRISTOPHER FREDRICO: The youngest of Earl Fredrico's eight children, twin to his sister Trillory. Chris was accused of stealing a magical Shard, stripped of his family name, and banished from North Raec. But on his journey to the border, he turned aside to follow the riddle quest.

ARNOLD FREDRICO: Chris's cousin and lifelong friend. Arnold completed his training and was made a knight a few weeks before Chris's banishment.

TERRIN OF XELL: Being of the forest people, Terrin is practical and level-headed. Haunted by spirits from a young age, she has a strong distrust or even fear of magic.

NORA OF YORC: Though the mountain people of Yorc are renowned for their strength and skill as warriors, Nora is shy and dislikes conflict. Taught herbal medicine by her aunt, she wants to become a healer, but she also enjoys history.

❧

Met on Their Journey

ANDREA: Nora's childhood friend, a harpy seer whose family guarded the first riddle. Andrea set the companions on their quest.

THOMAS: A skilled healer, forced into retirement after a dispute with the Healer's Guild. Thomas loves ancient stories, especially those of King Miles, and was researching the riddles when he met Chris and joined the quest.

CEIANNA: Second Sentry of Shylak, a soldier of the swamp people. Ceianna was raised by her grandmother to hate the forest people, but she became Terrin's friend and helped rescue her from the wraiths.

❧

The Fredrico Family

DIARD FREDRICO: Earl of Fredricburg, and father to Chris.

TRILLORY: Chris's twin sister, who has had water magic from childhood. Not a typical noblewoman, Trill would rather tend a garden than attend parties.

ANTHONY: The eldest son of Earl Fredrico. A favorite of Duke Grith, Anthony is always looking for more friends in high places.

GILLIAN: Second son of Earl Fredrico, Ambassador to South Raec.

SIR HENRY FREDRICO: Arnold's father, a renowned knight who tutored the Coric princes in swordsmanship.

❧

The Royal Family

NYLAN CORIC: King of North Raec.

TYLER: Crown prince of North Raec. Tyler presided over Chris's trial and banishment.

BRAYDEN: The second-born prince, sent as an emissary to South Raec. An awkward youth, Brayden prefers the quiet of a library over the bustle of court.

KING MILES: (*deceased*) Historic founder of the Coric Dynasty. Miles followed the riddle quest centuries ago and discovered the Riddled Stone, a magical artifact that is the emblem of the king's authority.

⌘

Other Characters

DUKE GRITH: Advisor to King Nylan. Grith has powerful magic, but hides it.

ERIC: The son of Duke Grith, and a fellow (though much weaker) magician.

MASON: Chamberlain of Castle Coric. Distantly related to the royal family, Mason handled much of Brayden's tutoring.

LADY JOLINE: Ambassador to North Raec from the Diamond Isles. Joline tutored Trillory in court manners.

KING ORIN D'RANG: Monarch of South Raec.

BARON TORC: A young South Raecan noble on King Orin's advisory council.

∾

PART ONE

∾

❧ 1 ❧

Arnold

The cold stone pressed against Arnold's shoulders, telling him he couldn't back any further into the corner. But that didn't stop him from trying.

Across the room, the monster didn't seem to have noticed him. Yet. But he was sure that it would soon. There could be no hiding from all those eyes, and it was almost finished with its previous prey.

Timmy, his friend and companion, lay crushed to a pulp beneath its hairy legs.

Arnold glanced at the door, wondering if he could make a run for it. But he remembered how heavy the thick, oaken door had been when he first entered the room, and from that side he had merely turned the handle and pushed. From this side, the fact he could barely reach the handle would make it hard to hang on while pulling.

His eyes flicked back to the monster. It just sat there, gloating over Timmy's lifeless body.

He would be next.

The bare, stone room gave him nowhere to hide. If fleeing was out of the question, he would have to fight his way out.

Taking a deep breath and balling his hands into fists, he took a step forward.

Or tried to. His foot scraped across the ground.

The monster skittered back, surprised.

"Never hesitate! Always press your advantage while you can." His father's words echoed in Arnold's ears.

But he was frozen. He couldn't take a second step.

"If your first plan falls apart, do not push it. Fighters must always be ready to reassess the situation at a moment's notice and adapt to the new circumstances."

Arnold reversed his step, going back to his corner.

His one advantage had been lost. The monster had already recovered. Now it shifted its weight back and waved its front legs in the air, preparing to strike.

He was dead. There was no way he could defeat the beast now.

"Hawks scream when fighting to remind their enemy that they are the stronger one, and to remind themselves. Both are important: If you think you've lost, then you already have. But the same is true for your enemy."

Right. If he was afraid, he should just turn the tables! Arnold opened his mouth, filling his lungs for the ultimate battle cry.

What came out was a long wail. It tore through the silence of the room—and through what shred of courage he'd worked up. His knees buckled beneath him, his shoulders slumped in defeat.

"Arnold?"

The door flew open, crashing against the wall. In the doorway stood his mother, her brow creased, her gray eyes filled with worry.

"Mama!" cried Arnold. "Don't come in! There's a monster."

"A monster?" She turned to scan the room. "You mean this?" In three strides she approached the creature, bent, and lifted it by its sides between two fingers.

"It's just a tarantula," she said. "It can't hurt you."

"But it killed Timmy."

"Timmy?"

Arnold's mother crouched to look him in the eyes.

"Who's Timmy?"

"My pet mouse." He pointed to Timmy's remains.

"I didn't know you had a pet mouse."

"He's been living here for a week, and I've been taking care of him. He was going to be my squire when I became a knight. But now…" He sniffed.

His mother sighed. "I'm sorry, sweetheart, I didn't know. Come here."

He rose and crossed the room, going round to stay on the opposite side of his mother from the tarantula, eyeing it warily.

His mother wrapped her free arm around him and pulled him close.

"I'm sure it was horrible for you to watch Timmy die. But you know a mouse and a human boy are two very different things. The tarantula cannot hurt you. Touch it and you'll see."

She held it up.

The sight of its eight legs flailing uselessly in the air made Arnold's stomach turn over, and he pulled away, shaking his head violently. Nothing had the right to that many legs. Especially such long, thick, hairy ones.

His mother sighed and released him. Then she turned, set the spider in the doorway and watched it scurry away.

"Why did you do that? It killed Timmy!"

His mother turned back to him, and took his shoulders in

her hands.

"Arnold, do you love animals?"

"Of course. You've always told me to."

"Well, that tarantula was just an animal. Like any other. It held no threat to us."

"It killed Timmy!"

"And we will mourn his loss, but the spider was only doing what it had to do to survive. It eats mice, and Timmy was a mouse. That's how it works with animals."

"But I loved Timmy. You told me I should love animals, and I loved Timmy."

"Sadly, no matter how much we love them, animals can become no more than what they are. Timmy was a mouse, and he lived the life of a mouse. He was only more than a mouse in your eyes, though I'm sure, in his own way, he valued your friendship. Now the only thing we can do for him is to give him a proper burial."

Mother released him and scooped up Timmy's body. "Do you think he'd like it if we put him under the rose bushes?"

Arnold sniffed. "He'd prefer lilacs."

"Of course."

Mother stood and led him through the halls of the fortress, out across the courtyard, and into the garden. Kneeling in front of the lilac bushes, she handed him Timmy.

"You hold him, and I'll make a grave."

Nodding, he cradled what was left of Timmy. It wasn't much. He watched as his mother's long slender hands cleared away the dirt.

"Melody?"

The gruff voice made Arnold jump.

"I was wondering where you were. What in the world are you doing?"

He turned to see his father looming behind him, his stern face creased with confusion.

"A tarantula killed Arnold's pet mouse, and we're burying it," Mother said calmly. She removed another scoop of dirt without even looking up.

"His pet mouse?" Father's dark, amber eyes narrowed. His lips pursed, stretching the skin to show a narrow, white scar. Arnold's father had many such scars. One at his jaw, another over his eye. He was even missing a chunk out of his left ear. All the scars showed clearly against his ruddy skin.

"Yes." Mother's voice sounded tense, but she continued to dig.

Arnold's spine stiffened. He could feel his father's irritation.

"What on earth is he doing with a pet mouse?" Father's voice had lowered to an ominous rumble. Experience taught Arnold that after this, the yelling would start.

He saw his mother's eyes slide shut as she prepared an answer.

He chose to interject, "His name was Timothy. He was going to be my squire one day."

"A squire? A mouse cannot be a squire. It couldn't even handle a little old spider! Even if it had the brains and strength to fight, it would be dead of natural causes before you are old enough to hold a real sword."

Arnold's hands closed protectively over Timmy's remains.

"There's no reason to honor such a weak animal. If it can't even protect itself, what is its purpose?"

"But he was my friend," Arnold murmured.

"Then you should have protected him. Now stop sobbing like an idiot and leave it be."

"Husband!" Mother snapped.

"The boy should face reality."

Melody stood and turned to meet her husband's eyes, flecks of fiery silver lighting her gray eyes. "I, too, think Arnold should be able to face reality. But he is only six. There is no reason he cannot mourn the loss of his friend."

"It was you, wasn't it? Putting ideas into his head about treating animals as equals."

"I have never said they should be treated as equals. Merely that they should be respected and cared for. They are as much a part of this world as we are, and essential to our way of life."

"That's one thing, but a mouse? Befriending a mouse?" Father's voice was rising. "That is foolishness!"

Arnold made a snap decision. He jumped to his feet, tossing aside Timmy's remains. "You're right, Papa. I should have known better than to care about a mouse. It won't happen again." He forced a smile as he raised his head to meet his father's eyes.

There was a momentary staring contest. Then his father said, "Good. Then wipe those tears, boy."

Arnold raised a hand to touch his face. It was wet and slick with tears he didn't know he'd been crying. He quickly wiped them away with his sleeve and laughed.

"I didn't even know I was crying. I must have gotten dust in my eyes, silly me."

He then turned and walked away. He rounded the corner, then stopped to listen.

"You're too hard on him."

"There's no excuse for a boy his age to be befriending mice."

"In your eyes. But he has no one else to be friends with."

"There are plenty of other boys here."

"Yes, but none his age. And they all look at him as your son. As someone to please for your sake. Not as someone they want a real friendship with."

There was a long silence.

Then Mother added, "You're visiting your brother in Fredricburg soon, right? Diard has a young son, too. You should take Arnold with you. It would be a good experience for him."

"Hmmph."

$$\text{\large ❦ 2 ❦}$$

Nora, 13 years later

Nora woke to weak morning light filtering through the leaves. She pushed back her blanket and sat up, wincing at the pain in her right leg. The soldier's sword had left a nasty gash, but it was a clean cut, and while it had bled heavily at first, it was healing well. She'd have an impressive scar, but she was in no immediate danger.

Except, the soldiers had recognized them.

So now the king knew they'd defied his decree of banishment.

And she had no idea whether her friends had escaped.

On the other side of the clearing, Minty raised her head.

Nora downed a hard biscuit and a strip of jerky, washing the dry-food flavor away with a swallow of water. Then she pulled out her bandages and medicine and crossed the clearing to tend her horse's wounds.

They couldn't risk infection. She'd seen what that had done to Arnold, losing his hand.

She swayed into Minty, unable to stop the tears that pooled

in her eyes.

Minty whickered, poking her nose against Nora's shoulder.

"I'm sure it's fine." She spoke gently, to sooth the horse. "I know I saw Terrin leave, and Ceianna was there to help. I'm sure the others got away, too." She cleaned each cut, tenderly spreading salve over the worst. "Nothing we can do now. We'll just follow the plan and head to River's Cross. Meet up, cross the Kaln, and then south to the cliffs— Easy, girl."

Minty jerked her head when Nora touched the largest cut. Then nickered again.

"You weren't even worrying about them, were you? You just want water, don't you? Give me a minute."

Nora stepped back, satisfied. Minty, too, was healing well.

❧

Arnold

Arnold popped the last bite of jerky into his mouth. He draped his arms across his knee, his right thumb gently rubbing the stump of his left hand. Out of the corner of his eye, he watched a sparrow perched on the back of his saddle. It pecked at the leather a couple times, then hopped sideways.

"You have to face it sometime," said Thomas as he shoved bandages into his pack.

"Huh, the bird?" Arnold blinked, then shook his head. "No, the saddle. Right." He sighed.

"Unless you don't think you're up to it?" the old man said with a grin.

"Me? Give in to a measly saddle? Never!" Arnold leaped to his feet and shook his fist. The bird fled.

Thomas laughed.

Rich looked up from his quiet grazing to give Arnold an odd look.

Arnold whistled as he strode to his saddle, and Rich trotted across the clearing. Thomas turned to saddle up his own horse.

"No holding your breath today," Arnold said, patting Rich's neck.

Now, to face the saddle. It was his first time tacking Rich up since losing his hand. When they were traveling together, Chris or Terrin always beat him to the task—and to tell the truth, he had let them pamper him. No longer.

First, he threw the saddle pad over Rich's back, shifting one side and then the other until it was in place. He bent over the saddle. Tilting it back with his right hand, he slid his left arm underneath and lifted. Throwing it across Rich's back was easy.

Now the challenging part. Reaching under Rich, he grabbed the girth and pulled it around. His eyes darted between the ring on the edge of the girth and the long leather strap he needed to tie to it. Awkwardly pinning the girth to Rich's side with his left forearm, he grabbed the end of the strap. As he poked it through the ring, Rich turned his head to stare at him, snorted, and shook his mane.

"If you have a better idea, I'd love to hear it," said Arnold. Holding the strap tighter than necessary, he released the girth. He wound the leather through the ring again, pulling it snug before tying the knot. He tied it as loosely as he could, but it still took a few tries to poke the end through.

Using his arm once more to brace himself against Rich, he started to pull the knot tighter. Rich glanced at him, then blew out a long stream of air, as if emptying his lungs.

"Thanks buddy," said Arnold, grinning.

He finished and stepped back. "Would you look at that. I *am* smarter than a saddle."

"Well done," said Thomas. He'd already finished tacking. "You still need a bridle."

"Right."

Arnold grabbed the bridle and started to pull it over Rich's ears. His left hand went to catch the bit, and he paused as his stump bumped against it.

His throat caught for a second and he met Rich's eyes. Rich blinked once, then opened his mouth and let Arnold slip the bit between his teeth.

"I don't know what I'd do without you, buddy," Arnold said, tossing the reins around the saddle horn.

"And, Thomas, if you ever need help with your saddle, I'd be happy to lend you a hand." Arnold grinned broadly. "Eh?"

Thomas shook his head. "The singular being key. You seem upbeat. I thought you'd be more worried about Terrin."

Arnold raised an eyebrow. "Terrin can take care of herself. Besides, she'd slap me if I even thought of worrying over her."

"Hmm," said Thomas, grabbing his bag and mounting his horse.

"What?" Arnold snatched up his own pack.

"Nothing, nothing. Though I wouldn't be surprised if she's worrying about you."

"Why would she do that? She's probably glad to be free of my jokes. No appreciation for fine humor."

As he mounted, he glanced at his stump.

Hand or no, I proved yesterday I'm still a decent fighter.

It wasn't the same, though. And in a full scale battle—

He shook his head.

No. There's no reason for anyone to be worrying about me.

❧

Terrin

"All right, let's get out of here," said Terrin as Chris finished his sandwich. She'd already saddled Leaf.

He took a sip of water before answering. "What's the big hurry?"

"Nothing. I just… don't want those soldiers to find us." She crossed her arms as Chris stood and started saddling Marc.

In reality, all she could think of was the previous night, when she had summoned a spirit. And though she didn't feel the slightest tingle of magic nearby, it felt like the trees were watching her.

When Chris finished, Terrin snatched up her pack and half-leaped towards Leaf.

The bag twisted in her hand, and the flap dropped open, sending her belongings tumbling across the ground. Leaf skittered sideways and reproachfully tilted her head towards Terrin.

Terrin took a slow breath as she knelt to repack her bag.

"What's wrong with you today?" Chris asked. "You've been out of it all morning. You even forgot to buckle your pack." He bent to gather a few items that had bounced a couple feet away.

"It's nothing, I'm just—" She paused as she pulled out the wraith-tooth knife from beneath a pile of clothing. She swallowed and shoved it into the pack.

The knife had scared off the spirit. It was her shield. But it reminded her of the sadness she'd sensed as the spirit drifted away.

"You're just?" prodded Chris. He held out her bundle of jerky strips.

She shook herself. "Worried about the others."

It wasn't a lie, exactly. Who knew what trouble Arnold would get into without Chris or her to keep him in line?

She turned away to tie the bag behind her saddle. "I'm surprised you aren't. Worried, that is. Isn't that your specialty?"

"After the speech you gave me yesterday? I wouldn't dare."

"Oh. Right," Terrin murmured. "Good. Still, we should get to River's Cross as soon as possible."

∻ 3 ∻

Brayden

The servant knocked seven times before Brayden could manage a thick, sleepy, "Okay, okay, five more minutes." And rolled over.

As he burrowed deeper into the pillow, a vague thought flitted through his mind. He had meant to wake up early hadn't he? But he was so tired…

He jerked up, sending his pillow flying across the room.

"Urragh," he groaned as his wounded arm twinged.

He remembered it all: the glint of moonlight on that wickedly curved knife, pain when the blade sliced into his bicep. His own knife slipping through the assassin's neck. The blood on his bedroom rug. No wonder he was so tired. He'd be surprised if he got four, or even three, hours of sleep the previous night. He just hoped he'd taken the man's body far enough away from the castle district that no one would tie it back to him.

But who had sent the assassin?

Who had tried to start a war?

Gillian Fredrico? The ambassador from North Raec hated him, Brayden was sure. But Gillian was no traitor. He wouldn't try to kill his own prince.

King Orin? The South Raecan monarch's desire for peace seemed sincere.

A South Raecan noble, perhaps that hot-headed Baron Torc? If it was one of the nobles, then there was a chance Brayden could figure it out by seeing their reactions to him.

That is, if he got to the palace before they would expect news of his death—

He jumped from bed, traces of exhaustion not quite forgotten, but outweighed by political matters. He had come here to keep a war from starting, and he intended to fulfill that mission.

He dressed quickly, placed the pillow back on the bed, and ran down the stairs, wondering if it would be reasonable for him to go straight to the palace and have breakfast there.

"Prince Brayden."

Ambassador Gillian Fredrico greeted him before he passed the dining room. Brayden slowed, dreading what came next. He stopped in the arched doorway.

He had hoped that the ambassador would still be asleep at this hour.

Gillian stood, both hands on the table as he leaned across, staring at Brayden.

"We need to discuss your behavior at the palace yesterday," said Gillian, straightening to cross his arms.

Brayden bowed his head. He might be a prince, but as the second son, he received little to no respect from other nobles of any rank. And he couldn't blame them. His brother Tyler had the bearing of royalty, even from childhood, while he was more likely to trip over his own feet.

"I thought we had that discussion last night," he mumbled.

Gillian humphed. "We did. But I'm afraid that I was in a sour mood, and I may not have expressed myself as clearly as was my intention.

"Although you disobeyed my instructions to remain silent during the court session, I admit that somehow you seem to have won King Orin's interest. I had originally intended to place you on the first boat back to Coricstead. But as it is, I will consider allowing you to stay for a marginally extended period of time, under certain conditions."

Brayden resisted the urge to roll his eyes. Gillian was certainly an experienced ambassador—experienced in long words and complicated sentences.

"What conditions?" He would agree to almost anything if it got him out of the house.

"First off, you must say nothing decisive. Ever. If it can possibly be helped, you should endeavor not to talk to anyone without my permission. I do not have time to train you in the finer points of diplomacy, so if you want to say something, consult with me first. If it is true that King Orin is set on negotiating a new treaty, then you must tell him that—"

"No."

Brayden wasn't sure what made him say it, but before he could think twice, the word popped out.

Gillian stopped and flushed. But he wasn't a horrible ambassador, and he managed a forced smile before saying, "Excuse me?"

Well, Brayden thought, *if I intend to do anything here, I have to follow through now.*

"I am a prince of North Raec. If I decide to stay longer than originally planned, you cannot stop me. If I decide to talk with someone, even the king, you cannot stop me. I accept full responsibility for any consequences my actions here may have, but I alone will be the judge of what those actions will be.

"When you next write to my father, you may ask him to order me back to Coricstead. But I will not go home until I receive such an order, or until I decide on my own that it is time."

He held Gillian's eyes, hoping that the ambassador couldn't hear his thudding heart.

The ambassador gritted his teeth. "It is one thing to say you'll accept the responsibility, and quite another to fulfill such a commitment. I must answer to King Nylan for whatever repercussion may ensue, and I cannot let you go off and do whatever you want—"

"If it will ease your worries, I will read all of my father's commands concerning your actions here. I will study your reports. I will listen to your counsel. But first I would like to eat breakfast and visit the palace again."

Gillian clenched his fists. "Perhaps first you should read the letter from your father regarding your purpose here."

"Did that letter anywhere state that Father ordered me not to do or say anything?"

"Not explicitly."

"Then, as I said, if you dislike my actions, you must appeal to my father."

Brayden spun on his heel and left. If he wasn't allowed to eat breakfast at the palace, then he'd go without, but sitting down to a meal with Gillian after that conversation would be unbearable.

❧ 4 ❧

Nora

"I've been here before! I'm sure of it." Nora pulled Minty to a sharp stop, examining the fallen log just in front of her. She was no forest expert, but she was certain she'd crossed paths with the same one not long before.

"How do the forest people keep all of these trees straight?" Nora muttered, as she turned Minty away. The last time, she'd gone around the log, so this time she cut to the left. North, she hoped. It was not the straightest line to River's Cross, but it was better than circling the same area for the whole morning.

She seemed to have made the right decision. They had only gone a few strides through the forest when the underbrush opened to reveal a deer trail. Nora clucked and Minty picked up a trot.

She hated to keep Chris waiting, to delay his quest. Andrea had warned of something terrible coming when she showed them the first riddle, and judging from the rumors they'd heard in the mountains, and the soldiers in the forest, a war would start soon.

When King Miles followed the riddles, hundreds of years ago, he'd found the Riddled Stone and used its power to end a horrible war. Nora didn't know what they would find, but it had to be important. And time was running out.

$$\infty$$

Arnold

"Suppose we should think about stopping for the night soon?" Arnold asked.

"We might stop at one of those farms over there," said Thomas, pointing across a few fields. "Most country folk are willing to welcome travelers, if only in hope of news."

"Well, a warm meal would be nice," said Arnold. "And a proper bed," he added with a smile. "Though they probably know more about current events than we do."

"We can certainly *hope* for a warm meal, but we shouldn't intrude too much," Thomas scolded.

"Fine, fine," said Arnold. But glancing at the sun that was already casting a reddish glow over the fields, he was sure they'd be in luck. He doubted anyone would refuse them if they arrived at the start of the evening meal. "Let's hurry though."

It took longer to reach the farms than Arnold had expected, since they needed to avoid treading on the freshly planted crops. But as they pulled near, he could see men still working in the fields closer to the buildings, which turned out to be several houses clustered together.

Good, thought Arnold, *we're in time for supper.*

The three men working closest together looked up and leaned on their hoes as the travelers approached. One said something that made the leftmost man shake his head.

They slowed their horses, and Thomas waved. Arnold almost

used his left hand to do the same, but stopped himself. Instead he nodded to the men and tucked his stump behind his leg where he hoped it wouldn't be so obvious.

The one who had shaken his head approached them. A middle-aged man, his hair salted with gray, with a ruddy face and calloused hands. "Welcome friends. I hope health and prosperity have accompanied your travels."

As Thomas returned a long-winded greeting, the smallest of the men—still a boy really—groaned. The third, little more than a boy himself, elbowed him and glared.

The spokesman sighed. "Excuse my son. He has little patience for… anything."

Thomas laughed. "It is fine."

Arnold caught the boys' eyes and winked, mouthing, "Me, too." The older boy raised his eyes in exasperation while the younger grinned.

"I am Leonard. This is my eldest son, Lenny," said the man, gesturing to the two boys. "And Michael, my youngest. I assume you're looking for a place to stay?"

"That would be nice, though we by no means wish to intrude. Just a spot in a barn will be fine."

Leonard shook his head. "No, no. You're more than welcome to stay at our house. The village isn't big enough for an inn, but my wife insists on making up for it, and she wouldn't dream of you staying anywhere less than a proper bedroom. And you're in luck. I imagine the evening meal will be ready soon."

"You're too kind. We have our own food and—"

Leonard held up his hands. "It's not the choice of any of us. My wife will force it down your throat if she has to. Besides, tonight is a village get-together. There will be more than enough food for everyone and their fifth cousin."

"I'm afraid I only brought my fourth cousin," said Arnold before he could stop himself.

Leonard pinched his eyebrows together, but Michael cut off any immediate response he might have made by bursting into laughter. Even Lenny seemed amused.

When Michael had regained control of himself, their father continued, "Anyway, you're welcome to head straight on to our house. It's the—"

The ringing of a bell interrupted him.

"Or, I guess we can take you ourselves," said Leonard, shaking his head.

Thomas chuckled, then dismounted. Following his lead, Arnold slipped off his horse's back. As he took a hold of Rich's reins to lead him to the town, Michael gasped.

All turned to the boy, and even in the late evening light, Arnold could see he was blushing. "Sorry, I stubbed my toe." He quickly looked away, but not before they could follow his gaze to Arnold's stump.

Lenny's mouth formed a small 'o', and Leonard started to say something, but Arnold laughed. "Stubbed toes: the only thing worse than dragon bites."

They walked on in silence. As they drew near the house, the door swung open and a plump woman stepped out, with a sparkle in her eyes and a warm smile.

Leonard said, "And this is May."

"Oh, hello, welcome," May said. "You must be so tired from traveling. Here, just put your horses in the barn. Let Julie get those bags for you so you can go wash up. Leonard asked you to stay the night, right? Sometimes he forgets how to be polite. But you must stay. You can't go much further tonight, and it gets so cold on the plains when the sun sets. This summer especially seems rather slow to warm up. And you're in luck, we're having a bit of a party tonight, nothing big, but there will be plenty of good food and some music."

As Julie took their bags, she whispered, "Mother used to dream of running an inn, until she realized she'd have to charge money."

⁊

The houses of the village were built in a rough circle, making a plaza around the community well. Each family spread a blanket or set up table and chairs near their own home, but immediately splintered and formed new groups.

A few women greeted May with a hug, teased her about inviting in strangers yet again, and dragged her and Julie off to join their gaggle. Leonard and Thomas joined the other farmers. Children scarfed down their food and started playing, darting to and fro and occasionally upsetting someone's drink.

Soon the sun disappeared. A bonfire was lit, and one man set to tuning a fiddle.

Arnold stayed where Leonard had set up his family's blanket, nibbling the last few of May's dumplings. He could hear the farmers' conversations, but his mind wandered. He was more interested in the children's games than whether the lingering cool spell would stunt the corn.

And when Thomas mentioned he was a healer, Arnold lost interest entirely as several farmers and a few of the wives surrounded him, seeking advice on anything from a child's fever to how to handle a breech birth in livestock, even asking about herbs to discourage mice.

Lenny and Michael sat nearby. Out of the corner of his eye, Arnold could see Michael watching him, nibbling his lip, and rocking in place a little. Lenny was staring across the plaza, a dumpling hanging from his limp hand.

"So, are you and Thomas adventurers?" Michael finally blurted out.

Arnold grinned. "Well, we've certainly had a lot of adventures."

Michael glanced toward his parents, though it was hard to see anyone clearly in the light of the leaping flames, then scooted closer and whispered, "How'd you lose your hand?"

"Michael!" Lenny hissed. "You know better than to pry."

Arnold laughed.

"It's fine. I don't mind. We were attacked by wolves coming over the mountains. One of them bit me, and the wound got infected."

"You came over the mountains?" Michael's eyes widened, turning reddish gold in the firelight. "Scar Range, right? Aren't there harpies? Did you get a good look at them?"

"Slow down, Michael, and think," Lenny said. "If he had, he'd be dead."

Arnold hesitated. He had, in fact, gotten a very close look at all kinds of harpies, even spoke with them. But he could hardly tell Michael and Lenny about that.

Still, he hated to disappoint Michael.

"Well," Arnold spoke slowly. "We did get attacked by harpies, actually." This made even Lenny's eyes round. "And we barely escaped. We got lucky really." Luck had certainly been a factor. Arnold shook his head and added, "I would not recommend ever fighting a harpy."

"What are they like?" Michael leaned forward, sucking his lower lip in anticipation.

"Terrifying. Even the children are large and dangerous. Their beating wings make it hard to focus. And their talons, they're maybe this long." He held his arms about two feet apart. "Curved and deadly."

"Whoa," said Michael. "I wish I could be an adventurer. Or a knight. I would give anything to be a knight."

"Don't be ridiculous, Michael," said Lenny. "A scrawny boy like you? You'd just get killed."

Michael's jaw clenched. "You'll see. Bobby said there's a war going to start soon. And I plan to be the first one out there fighting."

"Michael! Don't say things like that. You— You can't just run off to a war. I mean…" Lenny bit his lip. "They wouldn't want a sixteen-year-old boy fighting, anyway."

Michael crossed his arms. "The younger prince is sixteen, isn't he? I bet *he'll* be fighting."

"Not likely. I don't think he's even a proper knight yet."

"Well, he's a prince. Why'd he need the title of knight?"

Lenny chuckled. "From what I've heard, he's not much of a prince."

Arnold had heard stories of the worthless younger prince. His own father had once tutored both princes in swordplay. He'd complained, "The boy's as likely to cut off his own arm as his enemy's. And he has no guts." He winced at the memory. Regardless of personal ability, the boy was still a prince, and that ought to have earned him some respect.

But it said something worth considering that even common folk from the middle of nowhere had formed the same opinion.

Michael had not given up on his argument. "Well, just 'cause he can't prince right, or is only sixteen, doesn't mean he can't fight," he grumbled.

"I know someone who was knighted at sixteen," inserted Arnold.

"Really? Who?" said Michael.

Glad he'd distracted them from debating the prince's princeliness, Arnold gave his wording a second thought. A small lie would be better than giving away his identity. "Not that I ever met him. But I heard that Earl Fredrico's eldest son Anthony was knighted at sixteen."

And had I not gone to school, I would have beaten his record and made knight at fourteen, he added silently.

"See," said Michael, punching Lenny in the shoulder. "It's not impossible for a sixteen-year-old to fight."

Lenny scowled and crossed his arms.

"Still," said Arnold quickly, not wanting to lose all his favor with Lenny. "That was after a lifetime of training, and a big helping of talent on top of it. And war is a terrible thing. Having your life constantly on the line might sound like adventure, but if you experienced it, you'd miss home."

"You should listen to him," said Lenny. "I don't understand why you're so eager to get yourself killed."

"You wouldn't," snapped Michael. "You like living the same life, year after year. You have good friends, and a girl—if you'd ever ask her."

Here, Michael glanced pointedly across the plaza. Though Arnold couldn't make out who he was looking at, he followed on the new mood and gave a low whistle.

"Shut up," said Lenny. "I'll ask her when I'm good and ready."

"Well," said Arnold, smiling, "at least you know you like her. That's better than some people I've met. But don't wait too long. Time is gold, you know."

"That's not even what the saying means," muttered Lenny.

Michael and Arnold laughed.

❧ 5 ❧

Trillory

"Okay," said Eric. "Let's start with what you can already do. Have you ever tried anything besides water?"

"No," said Trillory. "I've never given my magic much attention."

Today was her first 'official' magic lesson, though Eric had already explained the basic concepts of how magic worked. They were in his small practice room, tucked away in an unused wing of his father's manor. Since the fire incident the other day, Eric had cleaned up most of the papers that littered the floor.

However, she noticed that he'd already pulled out several more sheets, which had drifted into the corners of the room. She'd have to take care of them later.

He pulled out a seat for her at the room's small table before going around to sit across from her. On the table was a tray holding a pitcher of water and two cups.

"That's not surprising," said Eric, setting the cups aside. "But I thought I'd ask, since your talent is so strong."

He lifted the pitcher and poured out some water onto the

platter, stopping just before it overflowed, and then set the pitcher with the cups.

"All right, then. Show me what you can do. What's the hardest thing you've ever pulled off?" He grinned, leaning on the table.

"It's not much," said Trill. "Just shaping a ball or loop of water, or pushing a splash around. But I'll try for something more interesting."

She waved her hand over the surface of the water. It followed her motion, rolling into a ball. She raised her arm, pulling the water up by the tendrils of magic that flowed from her hand. She shut her eyes for a second, thinking of what she wanted to create.

With a smile, she opened her eyes.

Guiding the ball with her hand, she threw it up into the air, and, as she twisted her wrist, it opened into an umbrella. She let it hover for a second, then with her left hand she pulled down water from the center of the disk, making a hollow pillar that spread slightly where it touched the platter.

Turning her right hand into a fist, she gathered the rest of the umbrella into a puffy, cloud-like shape.

She shut her eyes again, feeling the magic that filled the water. Thousands of threads twisting together, connecting her to each droplet like a puppeteer to his marionette. Concentrating on these threads, she split them and let them spread between her fingers. Then, pulling the threads taut, she let her hand burst open and flicked it up.

The vibration of the motion ran through the magic. Even before she opened her eyes, she knew her motion had done what she wanted.

The water at the top of the trunk had split into hundreds of droplets, floating motionless around it, bunched to look like leaves. With slow movements she merged some of them together to connect to the trunk and make branches.

"There," she said, glancing at Eric. Though the leaf droplets between them distorted his face, she could tell his mouth had dropped wide open.

"You're amazing. I mean… even if water's your natural magic… you just… That's your version of 'not much'?"

Trill blushed.

"Wait," she said. "I have an idea." She leaned sideways to look at him around the tree, careful not to move her hands. "Can you color water?"

"Well, maybe. I never thought to try."

"There's always a first time."

He stood silent for a moment. Then he hesitantly reached out to touch the trunk of her creation.

She tensed as the magic holding the water in shape trembled, but it held.

One drop at a time, magic fell from Eric's hand like dye, spreading over the tree, up the trunk and around the branches, turning them brown. At first, it made the water look murky, but he dripped another bit of magic, and as this one spread it added golden hues to the water.

When he finished the trunk, he touched the top of the tree. This time his brow furrowed as he focused, making the magic flow down, between, and around the droplets, giving them a vibrant green hue. He waited until the first color was done before adding a dash of lighter green.

This last bit of magic took longer than the others, and when it was done, he collapsed back into his chair with enough force to make it rock.

"It's ten times better now," said Trill. "I love your magic."

She could see his smile through the tree, though it had a

brownish hue.

He laughed. "Even I have to say that was pretty impressive. Well… I guess you can let the tree go."

Hearing the hesitation in his voice, Trill bit the inside of her cheek. Then she shook her head.

"No way am I destroying this. Tell me how to make it ice."

"You want to try that right now? While holding that much magic in place?"

"It won't be that hard, will it? I mean, ice is related to water, isn't it?"

"True…" Eric still hesitated. Then he shrugged. "Well, worst-case scenario: you let the tree go."

"If it splashes and makes a mess, I'll clean it up."

"I can't argue with that. Now, the chant is 'water to ice', but remember the words aren't the magic. They just help you focus. In fact—" He stared at a corner of the ceiling for a moment, then looked at her. "Since you need to hold the water in place, too, try the words 'standing water to ice'. And you'd better make sure all the leaf drops are attached to the tree, or they'll fall and shatter."

Trill felt a bit silly saying the chant, but she wanted to save the tree for at least a little while longer. "Standing water to ice. Standing water to ice."

She let her eyes slide shut, finding it easier to focus.

The new magic was slower than she was used to. Instead of the fluid, sweeping movements that controlled water, this magic crept from her hand, spinning out like a spider web or morning frost on a window.

The words became background noise as she followed the magic's progress. She had to shift the water-droplet-leaves so they would be connected to each other and to the tree. She flattened them out, giving them more of a leaf shape. And as the frosty magic spread over them, she tried to bend it so the threads made thin lines that would give the leaves veins.

When the magic fully covered the tree, she released it.

She hadn't realized the taut threads were holding her in place as well as the tree, and she fell back as they released her. She gasped and opened her eyes. A bead of sweat rolled down from her temple.

"I would say that now is a good time for a break," said Eric.

He set a cup in front of her. She hadn't noticed him filling it with water, but he must have done it while she was shaping the tree.

"Thank you." She took a long drink. "Magic hasn't worn me out like that before."

"It made for a great test of your abilities, though. And the tree is beautiful."

She glanced at it. The ice had given the trunk a rough texture, accented by the varying shades of brown. The thin leaves moved ever so slightly, like crystal hanging from a chandelier, and the ice trapped the light, making them almost glow.

"Do you think anyone will mind if we stay in here all day? At least until it melts."

He hesitated for a moment. "You'll be fine. Everyone's used to you being a hermit. But until Father comes back from the capital, I have management duties. But I'll stay for a couple hours."

"I suppose I forget that you actually have responsibilities." Trill laughed, though her heart sank. "I still haven't adjusted to how much busier Charlon is than Fredricburg. The tree won't last that long, anyway. It's pretty warm in here."

"It will last longer than normal ice would," he assured her. "It won't start melting until the magic fades. Or 'soaks in' might be the better term."

"Really?"

"I think. As long as the magic is present, it should hold the water in ice form. It might melt if we set a fire next to it, but at just room temperature, it should be okay."

Trill took another sip of her water, preparing herself for a real lesson before asking, "What about my shaping magic, that made it a tree in the first place? If I let it go, the water would have fallen back to the platter right away."

"That's different. You weren't changing the properties of the object, just moving it. Without you holding its shape, the magic just collapses, and the water escapes. You see, there are different types of magic, like—" He cut himself off and jumped out of the chair.

Trill watched as he crossed to the bookshelf and grabbed some of the sheets of paper stuck at random between books. He shuffled the papers around and tilted a couple of books to look behind them. Finally, he pulled out a badly bent quill pen.

He attempted to straighten it, then shook his head. Sitting, he started writing. His words flowed from the pen in scribbled swirls. He barely lifted the tip, even when he made mistakes. The pen skated across the page around the correct words to scratch out the wrong ones, or to make notations.

It was relaxing to watch. Trill finished her cup of water.

When he'd filled the first page, his eyes skimmed over it. Then in one motion he pulled it into his hand and crumpled it while still holding the pen. He tossed the ball of paper, eyes already locked on the next page. The ball bounced off the wall and disappeared behind the bookshelf. Eric was already writing on the second sheet. This time, he seemed more confident, scratching out only a few words, and he no longer notated.

"Done."

He dropped the pen to the side, and it rolled off the table.

Eric ignored it and handed her the paper.

She took it, now understanding how the room had become such a mess. But before she could read it, Eric launched into an animated speech, his eyes twinkling.

"While all magicians have something they have an affinity for—you with water, and me with color—which is easier for them to work with, magic in general has two main types.

"*Flowing magic,* for example, is what you use to manipulate water. It is a magic that connects us directly to the object we're affecting. We pull the magic from within ourselves as we need it, but if the connection is broken, then the magic will dissipate, losing its hold on the object. Shaping something, like your water, is one example of this. And also summoning—making something new, like fire, from solid magic—and controlling people, I think.

"*Standing magic* is what you used to transform the water into ice, or what I use to change the color of something. This type of magic doesn't connect to the caster as flowing magic does. Instead it attaches to the object, slowly soaking in and making a permanent change. Standing magic doesn't have to be continually sustained. You give your spell the magic it needs at the time of casting, and then it stands on its own. This would include changing an object's properties, healing magic, and some other random spells like teleportation."

When Eric stopped, he surprisingly didn't gasp for breath, but instead took one long sip of water before relaxing.

Trill's lips twitched, and she waved the paper. "Why did I need this, if you were going to say all that?"

"I— well, I'd never really thought about it before, so I figured I should write it down, and then..." he trailed off.

Trill frowned, thinking. "Isn't there some, say, flowing or manipulation magic that doesn't dissipate?" she asked.

She had not yet told Eric that she thought magic had been involved in framing her twin brother for stealing the Shard, a fragment of the king's famous Riddled Stone. It had disappeared during a party at their home in Fredricburg, and Chris had been banished for the theft. She couldn't remember the party clearly, which worried her. But she thought she had sensed magic.

If controlling people was a flowing magic, it shouldn't have a permanent effect. Wouldn't her memory return when the magic faded?

"Well," Eric answered, "You can store most magic types in objects. That's how charms are created. It takes a lot of practice to make a charm, but they have the advantage of being usable at any time by anyone—even someone with no magic of their own—as long as they have enough power in them."

Not what she asked, but it might explain how Anthony did it. *If* he did it.

"But if I wanted to, say, wipe someone's memories?" She shrugged. "That would be manipulation magic, right? But there wouldn't be much point if it wasn't permanent."

"I don't know much about memories," he said. "But when you move water from one bowl to another, it stays there. The magic might fade, but the water wouldn't move back."

❦ 6 ❦

Nora

After the deer trail ran out, the forest seemed thicker than ever. Only the slightest dappling of sunlight fell through the leaves. Nora had given up and made camp for the night. When she awoke the next morning, she thought for a moment it was still dusk.

"How do the forest people tell direction when they can barely see the sun?" she grumbled as she packed up her bedroll. "I'm buying a compass next chance I get. What do you think, Minty? Which way is east?"

Minty, tied to a nearby tree, turned her head as much as she could and snorted.

"I don't have a clue either," Nora leaned down to grab Minty's saddle.

As she straightened, a strong wind cut through the forest, whipping her long blond hair around her head. She squeezed her eyes shut to protect them from the strands of hair that cut at her face.

When the wind stopped, she set the saddle down to wipe the

tears that had sprung to her eyes. She was used to winds like that in the mountains, but she would have thought the trees would block them.

A thunderous crack reverberated through the forest. Nora jumped, losing her balance and falling to the ground.

Minty jerked back and reared, snapping the lead rope loose from her halter. Her front hooves thrashed in the air. Her eyes shone white, and her ears were pinned back. As soon as her hooves thudded back to the ground, she broke into a run, disappearing into the trees.

"Minty, stop! Whoa. Whoa. Stop, Minty!"

Nora scrambled back to her feet. She tried to run after her horse, but within minutes, the sound of hooves faded away.

"Minty! Come back, Minty."

Her words echoed among the silent trees.

Making a sound between a growl and a groan, she struck the side of her fist against the nearest trunk. She winced and cradled her hand as she turned to go back to her camp.

With a sigh, she sat back against an oak tree, considering her options. The horse had been her companion for three years, a gift from Chris. Even if there was a way to catch up with her friends on foot, she couldn't imagine abandoning Minty.

It was unlikely the horse would find her way back through the woods. But Nora knew the general direction Minty had gone, and the horse would calm down soon.

She picked up the lead rope, assessing the damage. Its hook was bent, but she could probably still use it. Putting it in her bag, she glared at the saddle. Though she would have a hard time finding it again if Minty had gone far, she couldn't carry it through the woods.

She decided to leave it where it was. There was no point in

trying to shield it from the elements. Tucking it under a bush would only make it harder to find.

If she had to ride bareback, fine.

Swinging the pack over her shoulders, she turned to follow her horse.

❧

Christopher

Chris's stomach twinged with hunger, but he was reluctant to stop for lunch. He and Terrin had fled southward after the battle, then turned east until they reached the edge of the forest. That would have been fine if they wanted to go straight to the coast. But it put them well out of their way for the rendezvous.

Now the plain stretched away to the north, and he hoped the others were out there, safely on their own way to River's Cross.

His stomach rumbled.

"I heard that," said Terrin.

"I'm not that hungry," said Chris, "I was just… thinking about the cakes the school cook used to make. I should think about horse manure or something like that instead."

"Those cakes were hard as tack. Horse manure would almost be an improvement."

Chris gagged at the thought of eating horse manure. *At least she's in a better mood today.* "Well, my appetite is now ruined."

"Mine isn't," said Terrin with a grin. "Besides, weren't you the one saying we should enjoy meals while we can, since we'll restock in town?"

"Well…"

Chris glanced around. In the distance, he could just make out a cluster of farm buildings. "Fine, we'll have lunch. But first we should make sure we're at least going the right way."

"Do you not trust my geography skills?"

"You're starting to sound like Arnold," said Chris. "But the straighter line we take, the sooner we'll get there. That town looks big enough they might even have a map. And riding that far will give me time to forget about manure cakes."

Terrin laughed. "True. But on a serious note, what if those soldiers have already broadcast the news that Honorable Christopher Fredrico has failed to obey his banishment? Going there could be dangerous."

Chris shook his head. "Unlikely. Those soldiers should have gone straight to the king. This wouldn't have been on their way to Coricstead, so it will be safe. And if it's not, then River's Cross won't be safe either."

If those *were* North Raecan soldiers. Chris didn't know what else they could be, but they had seemed strange.

To distract himself from his worries—and from manure cakes—he mused over the words of the last riddle.

> "Air rushing, rushing by,
> Faster, faster than the eye.
> Far above the deep, deep blue,
> Where water dashes at the rocks.
> And higher still the great one flies,
> Guarding hope as watchmen pose."

They had decided the clue described an oceanside cliff. Arnold remembered hearing about boulders that looked like men at Dawncliff, on the southeastern coast.

Chris didn't come up with any new ideas, but thinking helped to pass the time, and an hour later, they were riding up to a group of farmers at work.

"Hello, friends," called Chris. "We are traveling to River's

Cross, and we're wondering if you knew the quickest way?"

"Hmm," the man rubbed his chin. "Around the north-east edge of the fields, there's an old grove of sycamores. If you strike out from the eastern side of town and ride straight through them, I imagine you'll be on a direct line."

"Thank you," said Chris, nodding his head.

One of the men elbowed his companion. "If you haven't had lunch yet, I'd recommend heading down to that house over there."

He pointed, and the others snickered.

"What's the joke?" said Terrin, her eyes narrowed.

"Oh, it's not on you," said the first man. "The missus there likes to take in travelers, feed them, offer them a place to stay and all, much to the annoyance of her husband. We like to tease him about it. But he doesn't really mind. And the food is good."

"Thank you for the advice," said Chris. "What do you think, Terrin?"

"Well, I am hungry."

They were still a couple hundred feet from the house when a woman came out, waving at them.

"You're just in time for lunch," she called. "Julie! Come, show these people where to put their horses."

A girl on the edge of adulthood popped out from behind the house. She waved to them and jogged over as they dismounted, her light brown hair bouncing merrily.

"Mother didn't even ask you first, did she?" she said and laughed. "I assume one of the other families sent you our way?"

"Yes. Sorry if it's an inconvenience, but the offer of food was hard to pass up," said Chris.

"Oh, it's fine. We have enough to spare. Father will huff about it, but he loves visitors just as much as Mother does. He wouldn't put up with it otherwise."

Julie led them to the stables and fetched water and feed for the horses while Chris and Terrin rubbed them down. They were just finishing when a man and two boys appeared around the house.

"I see my wife's invited people into my house without asking, once again," the man grumbled.

"Sorry. We'll leave if you want," said Chris.

"That's what they all say. But once you're here, there's no getting out of May's grasp. Come in, come in. The boys will finish taking care of your horses. I'm Leonard, this is Lenny and Michael. You've met Julie and May."

Michael stared at Terrin. "You're a forest person, aren't you?" he asked.

Leonard smacked the back of his head. "Don't be rude, Michael. Excuse him. Too curious for his own good."

Michael pouted, but as the older men moved away, he whispered, "What's it like living in the forest?"

Terrin whispered back, "Not so different from how you live, except we hunt instead of farm."

She turned toward the house, but over her shoulder she added with a grin: "And we listen to our elders."

❧ 7 ❧

Arnold

The door of the room clicked shut after Thomas, leaving Arnold alone in the dingy room of the small, cheap inn at River's Cross. The old man had gone to search for a place to wash their clothes—something much needed—and to find out where they might buy rations.

Except Arnold wasn't alone. He glanced over to the upper corner of the room, filled by a spider web. A spider web with a nasty, fat spider plopped in the middle. Arnold shuddered.

Keeping one eye on the spider, Arnold bent to grab his sword, which he had set by his bag. He drew it slowly from its sheath with a satisfying hiss.

"Okay, little monster. We can do this the easy way, or the hard way. Let's save each other some heartache and go with easy," said Arnold, pointing the sword at the spider.

He took slow steps towards it until the tip of the blade was just shy of the web. Setting his feet wide and taking a deep breath to brace himself, he swished the blade forward and up beneath the spider. Without pausing, he spun, still holding the blade away from him, and lowered it.

On the end of the sword sat the spider, crouched low, clinging with its eight spindly legs.

"So far, so good. Just stay there," said Arnold, taking a step towards the door.

The spider burst forward, dashing up the blade. Arnold jerked the sword in surprise, and the spider flew off.

It landed a few feet away, on its side and motionless.

After staring it down for a second, Arnold took a step towards it, hoping it was dead. At his movement, the spider sprang back to life, flipping itself back over and skittering towards the bed.

"Oh, no, you don't," Arnold said, swinging his sword down across its path to herd it towards the door, careful not to scratch the worn floor.

The spider crawled straight over the blade, and even when Arnold tried to lift it away from the floor, it jumped clear and continued on its way. It disappeared between their two packs.

"Drat."

Arnold gingerly caught the strap of Thomas's bag with the tip of his sword and tossed it across the room. When this revealed no spider, he did the same with his. Again no luck.

"You went under the bed, didn't you?" Arnold groaned. "Why did you pick the hard way? I'm sure you'd rather live, and I don't want to kill— Well, no, I would love to just kill you. But I'd rather spare you."

He crouched down to peer under the bed. Sure enough, he could make out the glint of two or three of the spider's eight eyes.

Arnold crawled towards the bed, eyes locked with the spider's, his grip tightening around his sword's handle. Then, turning the blade sideways, he slashed beneath the bed in an arc, hoping it would have enough force to slice the spider in two.

Instead, the spider fled away from the approaching metal.

Out from under the bed.

Straight towards him.

Arnold scrambled away, choking on a stifled yelp. He kicked at the creature, and it turned towards the door.

Jumping to his feet, he circled around it and jerked the door open, swinging his blade over the spider. This time, his attempt to corral the monster was successful, and it exited the room. He slammed the door shut and collapsed to the floor, panting.

"I hate spiders," he muttered. Then he dragged himself to his feet and went to place the bags back next to the bed. Though his sword was technically still clean, he pulled out a handkerchief and wiped it down—just to be sure—before re-sheathing it.

❧

The evening passed slowly in the inn. The next morning they ate a quick breakfast and went straight back to their room.

"That might not have been the tastiest breakfast ever, but I still wish I could have had twice as much," Arnold said, throwing himself backwards onto the bed. "I'm going to miss eating fresh food when we leave."

"Me, too," said Thomas. He sat on a long bench under the room's single small window—nothing more than a hinged board that could be propped open or tied shut as needed. It was open now, and Thomas leaned out of it. "And a proper bed."

Though the inn didn't offer rooms with two beds, for a bit extra they'd dragged in a second mattress. Well, mattress was a generous term. It was a mound of straw wrapped in cloth, comfortable enough except that the straw stuck through the worn cloth, pricking you no matter how you lay.

Still, it was better than sleeping on the ground.

"Resting in the lap of luxury, aren't we? Even so, I hope the others get here soon." Arnold shut his eyes. "I feel useless just waiting."

He'd tried picking up a conversation with the locals the night before, but they just gossiped about the possibility of war with South Raec, and he and Thomas were the only travelers.

Thomas stood, stretched, and grabbed his pack. "Last night I told a few locals I'd look at their animals. I should be back soon."

"That's a natural healer for you. Have fun."

Arnold sat up to watch Thomas leave. Then he buckled his sword to his belt and headed out to the barnyard. If nothing else he could practice his swordplay.

It still felt weird to swing the blade one handed. Thomas had explained that his left hand factored into his balance and movements—the technical term went over Arnold's head. He worked through several standard forms with the sword first. Then a few mock fights, imagining and countering what a foe might do, or practicing how to react if his own slashes were countered.

It was almost lunch time when Thomas peeked around the corner of the barn with a smile. Arnold stopped mid-swing to look over at him.

"Chris and Terrin are here," Thomas said, stepping aside to let the two pass.

Arnold grinned, lowering the sword. "You made it!" He paused. "What about Nora?"

Chris shook his head, "We were hoping she was with you."

Brayden

Brayden had spent the morning after his fight with Gillian searching out every South Raecan noble he could find. They'd sneered at him, sidled away, or even left the room to avoid his presence.

But none seemed surprised to see him alive.

Then a secretary had found him and scheduled the meeting King Orin had requested. He had poured over Gillian's ambassadorial notes in preparation. They didn't really help.

As he sat across a desk from the king, sweat condensed on the palm of Brayden's hands, and a bead of it ran down the back of his neck. The secretary sat in a corner taking notes, with his glasses wobbling on the tip of his nose and a quill tickling the bottom of his chin.

"I'm glad you could remain in South Raec longer than expected," King Orin said. "I was looking forward to a chance to talk with you one on one."

Brayden nodded. He felt like he would fumble any words he

said, but he had to be polite. "I am also pleased. The idea of a new treaty intrigues me."

Thank goodness, his voice didn't break.

"I had been mulling over the idea for quite some time," said the king. "But if a South Raecan group is trying to stir up strife, then I believe now is the time to act. Perhaps our last chance to strengthen the bonds between our two countries. And to be honest, I am glad I can go over this with a member of the royal family, instead of just the ambassador."

Orin paused, as if considering his next words.

"Truthfully, Brayden, when you first arrived I expected little. But your youth is misleading. The way you handled the argument the other day… I can see why your father sent you."

Brayden forced a smile. He didn't know why his father had decided to trust him, but he was sure it had nothing to do with his political skills.

"The other day… that wasn't really— It was luck."

The king shook his head. "In this line of business, there's no such thing as luck. When things go wrong, we must take full responsibility, deserved or not. Therefore, for the sake of balance, we should also take responsibility for what goes right."

Brayden nodded. "I'll remember that."

"Now, about that treaty," said Orin. "The agreement we currently have is merely the cease-fire from the last war. That was a generation ago, almost two. It is more than time we make a permanent peace.

"First, I believe that we should embrace our relationship as sister countries. I've been studying the events leading up to, during, and after the original war that split our lands. I think it was never a matter of the South disliking the North, but rather that the countries had grown too big to be properly managed under a single monarchy. Taking inspiration from the Yorc treaty, I would like, therefore, to form a mutual defense pact. Should war unjustly come to your country, we would offer whatever aid we could to your defense, and you likewise to us."

Orin's mellow voice calmed Brayden. Even the secretary relaxed enough to adjust his glasses.

"Also, I've taken note that while peace treaties are often sealed with marriage agreements, this tradition has done little good. Later generations just use them as an excuse for one side of the family to demand sovereignty over the other. To avoid splitting loyalties in that way, we should make it illegal for a North Raecan—even the king—to own South Raecan land, and vice versa.

"And finally, I want to write a free trade agreement, including measures to encourage travel. I hope that if our people can get to know each other, the bloodlust between them might be lessened."

Brayden rubbed his hands together. Many times he'd considered ways to strengthen the peace between the countries. He was surprised to hear several of his own thoughts coming from King Orin's mouth.

"All of those ideas sound good in concept," he said. "But how they work in reality will depend on the details. A phrase like 'unjust war' is vague, certain to cause arguments over its interpretation. And if there are cross marriages where both parties own land, what would happen to the estates?"

King Orin grinned. "I knew you were a bright lad."

❧ 9 ❧

Nora

Nora had not found Minty, though she'd been walking more than a day. But she hadn't given up yet. She had no reason to, since she was lost herself.

Besides, the earth in this part of the forest was soft, and it was easy to follow the horse's tracks.

So Nora trekked on. Her back complained from the weight of her pack, and her legs, especially the right, were sore from all the walking. But none of her wounds had reopened. And she was used to climbing mountains, so she knew her limit was still far off.

The forest felt stranger than before. The trees pressed closer together around her, almost lining the path that Minty was taking. And the woods were quiet, stiller than seemed natural. What animal noises she could hear sounded distant. Occasionally a few leaves rustled, but she didn't feel a breeze.

The loudest noise came from the twigs and brush that crackled under her boots, which were made for protection against the hard stones and loose gravel of the mountains, not for silent movement through trees.

Nora rounded a bend in the strange path and caught the flicker of light ahead, just a pinprick through the trees.

Relieved, she scrambled over a root and, despite her leg, picked up a jog. The light grew rapidly. After a few seconds, she broke out into a clearing. Though blinded, she spread out her arms to bask in the sunlight, taking deep breaths.

"Finally! I thought those trees would never end. I'm sorry, Terrin, but I think I will avoid forests for the rest of my life."

Then she blinked her eyes and examined her surroundings.

Her heart fell.

The clearing was large, but twenty yards from her the ground dropped away. Along the distant horizon, she could see the northern mountains, her home. Minty's hoof prints led straight to the edge. Nora followed them, but even before she looked over, she knew this must be the Dark Forest cliff.

Below her, a sea of leaves stretched far enough to disappear into the haze. From the top, the Dark Forest didn't look too bad, just as thick and green as any other forest, but she didn't have to be of the forest people to feel the aura of death around it.

She shuddered.

A switchback trail dropped steeply at first, but then wound gradually down the cliff-side. Though the ground was harder here, it was clear that Minty's tracks went down.

"Why would you go there?" Nora whispered.

Even if the forest's deathly aura wasn't enough to keep animals away, why would Minty attempt such a treacherous path?

Nora sat, slipping her bag from her shoulder. The only good news was that she was no longer lost. If she followed the top of the cliff, she'd reach the plains, and then she could make her way to River's Cross.

But that would mean forsaking Minty to the Dark Forest.

The Dark Forest was the most infamous place in North Raec. Nothing was really known about it, except that even the forest people didn't dare travel there. She'd heard a variety of legends, though, and none were good.

If she went down the cliff, she'd no doubt become more lost. Who knew what dangers awaited her, or if Minty was even—

Nora winced at the thought. Her nails dug into her palms.

But the idea of giving up on Minty squeezed her chest to the point where she couldn't breathe, so there was no choice. With a resigned sigh, Nora once again lifted the pack to her shoulders and started the long climb down.

"Legends are just legends, right?" she said. But her adventures the past couple of months had taught her otherwise.

For the first few yards, Nora had to brace herself against the cliff wall to keep from slipping, but by the time her head was beneath the cliff top, the path had evened out. Even so, she'd not reached halfway when she had to stop to rest her leg.

Looking from here, she noticed that the forest was not as rich as it had first appeared. Dotted among the vivid greens were browns, even blacks, she thought. The aura seemed different, too. Not so much death as just deep sadness. Still, not something she wanted to go anywhere near.

She took a gulp from her water skin. "There's no turning back now," she said as she climbed to her feet and continued her descent.

The switchback path was much longer than it looked from above, and three quarters of the way down, her legs began to shake. She hadn't walked this many hours in one day since before school had started last fall.

School. That feels like years ago, Nora thought with a silent laugh. *I hope Mom and Dad aren't too worried about me. But...*

I don't regret running off with Chris and the others. Not even after everything that has happened. Maybe because of everything that has happened.

She reached the bottom without a second stop, but immediately checked her leg. Red had tinged the bandage. Grimacing, she knelt to untie it and apply more of her medicine. She didn't have much left, and her water skin was getting low, too. She'd had no chance to refill the latter, and she hadn't thought about the former.

Bandage secured, she stood and faced the trees. Though they were spaced apart, the canopy let no light pass, and the forest was heavily shadowed. The tree trunks were thick—though nothing like the trees she'd seen in the swamp—but they were a sickly gray. From here the blackened leaves were even more evident, but the ground seemed clear of any plants or debris.

With a deep breath, Nora took her first steps into the Dark Forest.

❧ 10 ❧

Trillory

The rattling of carriages, the smells of many shops and the bustle of people. Trill turned in a full circle, not wanting to miss anything in the busy streets of Charlon. She stopped, facing Eric. "You have no idea how long I've wanted to see the city from this angle. No offense, but it's much better than the view from the manor."

Everything felt so alive, a refreshing change from the halls of Duke Grith's manor, which seemed pretentious and stuffy when they were filled with nosy minor nobles and dreary now that most of the people had left.

Eric laughed. "The streets aren't too noisy for you? I thought you liked quiet."

Trill shook her head. "Quiet is nice, but seeing the same thing day after day, not so much. My legs needed a proper stretch. Besides, the noise of a city isn't so bad. No one trying to stick their nose in your business, or drag you to balls where you have to talk and dance with people you barely know and don't particularly like."

"I'm hurt. I didn't realize I was such poor company."

"Eric! I didn't mean you, you're—" Trill stopped, seeing the grin on Eric's face.

She flushed and tried to stammer something—even she wasn't sure what—but Eric had grabbed her arm and was pulling her through the crowd.

"Come on, I want to show you this shop. It has the most stunning cakes, in both taste and design. If I didn't know better, I'd say they used magic."

Trill ran to keep up, surprised by how easily he wove through the crowds. She'd always spent a lot of her day in the city, but her home of Fredricburg was not as bustling as Charlon. She was sure if Eric let go, she'd lose him in seconds.

Three streets later, they slowed to a stop in front of a wooden door, painted bright red. A worn sign swung overhead, bearing the picture of a cake, but the delicious aromas filling Trill's nose were more than enough identification. She breathed deeply.

Eric released her arm to open the door.

A glass counter filled with cakes and other treats divided the room. Light flooded the space through arched windows, beneath which ornate maple tables and chairs sat. Several paintings decorated the walls.

A boy in his upper teens sat behind the counter. He'd been leaning against it, half asleep, but he perked up as Trill and Eric entered. "Sir Eric!" He jumped to his feet and bowed. "I was beginning to think you'd forgotten us."

"How could I? You make the most delicious cakes I've ever had."

The boy grinned. "Keep talking like that and Mother will start feeding you for free. Who's this with you today?"

"A friend. Trill, meet Tom."

Trill smiled warmly and nodded to the boy. "Nice to meet you, Tom."

"Same. Any friend of Eric's is a friend of ours. I'll tell Ma you're here. I'm sure she'll be out in a sec." Tom hopped to his feet and disappeared through a door at the back of the store, letting in a wave of heat that filled the room.

"It's a beautiful shop," said Trill. "You seem to be a regular here. You aren't one of those people who can eat tons of cake without getting fat, are you?"

Eric laughed.

The door swung open and Tom reentered the room, followed by a woman who must be his mother. Small, with the well-muscled arms of a working woman. Her reddish brown hair was pulled into a bun, though several wisps had escaped. A rainbow of colored icing and bits of dough had splattered across her dark brown apron.

Her face split with a wide smile. "Eric! I've missed you. I trust you've prepared more praises for my treats?"

"He has," said Tom.

His mother bopped the back of his head. "I didn't ask you."

Eric laughed. "I've not only prepared my praises, Madame Camilla, but brought someone new to give you honor."

The baker looked Trill over and beamed. "Aren't you a pretty thing. Come, come. I'll fix you something special."

"There's no need," Trill said.

"No, no. I insist. I'm sure Eric will be the gentleman and pay."

"Of course," he said. "How could I not, when I'm the one who dragged her here in the first place."

"Yes, yes," said the woman, beckoning Trill over to the display case. "See? Now, what do you like in your cakes? Strawberries?

Nuts? Anything here is an option. I'll have it baked in a jiffy."

"I really don't—" Trill stammered.

"Is there anything you don't like?" asked Eric.

"Not particularly."

"Then, how about we just let the maestro work her artistry. She works best without boundaries anyway."

The woman bobbed her head. "Good, good. Give me an hour. No interruptions, Tom," she added as she exited to the kitchen.

ঔ

For the next hour, Eric led Trill past stalls overflowing with bright fabrics, through the shop of a master painter, and down a whole street devoted to selling flowers—which to Trill smelled as good as, if not better than, the cake shop.

At the appointed time, they once again stood in front of the bakery.

"Mama, they're back!" shouted Tom as they entered. To them he said, "Grab a seat, it'll just be a sec—" The door burst open behind him, and his mother appeared. She held a platter, and on that platter was a three-tiered cake, covered in artful icing.

Trill couldn't take her eyes off it, even as she sat in the chair Eric pulled out for her. Without letting it so much as wobble, Camilla crossed the room and set it in front of them.

"It's beautiful," breathed Trill.

Light green icing coated the cake, and black stems wove around the sides of each layer, tipped by delicate orange flowers. But most stunning were the chocolate flowers that topped each layer, so lifelike they would fool a bee.

"I told you," said Eric.

"But, how?" asked Trill.

The woman grinned and winked. "That's for me to know and

you to not find out. But how it looks is not nearly as important as how it tastes."

Tom appeared beside his mother, holding two plates, two forks, and a knife.

"How did you know I liked flowers?" Trill asked as the boy set a slice of the beautiful cake in front of her.

"Your dress was the first hint."

Trill looked down and laughed. She'd forgotten she was wearing the orange dress Eric had colored for her.

Her first bite of the cake was a burst of orangey sweetness that dissolved away like winter's first frost.

"Eric wasn't exaggerating. Are we sure you don't use magic?" Trill asked.

The woman guffawed. "No magic here. I have no time for such nonsense."

Eric caught Trill's eyes for a second and they both grinned.

The door swung open, and a man entered.

"Enjoy your cake, dear." Camilla patted Trill's shoulder, then turned to greet her new customer. "Ah, Emile, I didn't expect you back so soon. What can a woman like myself do for you?"

"Not enough," the man grumbled.

"Tosh. I find there's very little that a good cake can't fix. What's wrong?"

"That arrogant duke of yours still hasn't lifted the travel ban on South Raecan merchants. I've been here two weeks longer than intended. My stock's run out, and now I'm losing money just to live comfortably. Money I can't earn back. And do you think your blasted duke will reimburse me? Pah, he probably won't even apologize."

Trill stared at the cake, her good mood gone. Over the weeks she'd spent with Eric, she hadn't thought much about the possible war. She remembered Duke Grith placing the ban on merchants leaving the city, but she had assumed it was long ago lifted.

Eric's chair scraped back as he stood. Trill looked up, wondering how he'd take his father being insulted.

"It's about time we left," he whispered. He went to the counter and dropped a few coins. "You know where to send the rest of the cake, madame. It was delicious, as always."

ॐ 11 ॐ

Terrin

Terrin sat on the bench, curled against the wall. To one side, Chris paced the room. To the other, out the window, Arnold had dragged Thomas into a duel—the older man had already lost six times.

Though she hid it well, worry gnawed at Terrin's heart. What was keeping Nora from River's Cross? Despite her Yorc heritage, the mountain girl was an intellectual, not a fighter. Determined, yes, and talented, but easily the weakest of the five. Terrin hated to think what might have happened to her after the battle in the forest.

She also hated that it fell to her to be the voice of reason. She'd accepted the role readily at the start of the quest. Now it made her stomach twist.

But they had to move on.

She shifted to sit properly on the bench, preparing her speech.

Across the room, his back to her, Chris stopped pacing. "No matter how worried about Nora we are, we can't wait here forever.

Money is running low, and staying in one place too long isn't safe for me."

Terrin stared at Chris's rigid back. She hadn't expected this from him. He was usually very protective of Nora.

"Chris—"

"No. I know you would have said it, eventually. We have to finish our quest. We'll leave tomorrow morning. I'll write up a note for the innkeeper to give Nora when she catches up."

He turned to face Terrin. "Could you tell Arnold for me? He's more likely to see the reasoning if it's from you."

"Of course." She jumped to her feet, but before she left the room, she gave Chris a quick hug. "I know it was a hard decision. I'm proud of you."

છ

Nora

The Dark Forest was true to its name. So little light filtered through the leaves that the world seemed a dark gray. She could not make out the canopy above, and, despite being in a valley, the cold air nipped her skin.

It was unlike any other forest she'd known. The ground was too even, the trees too uniform and spaced far enough apart that she could see for dozens of yards. Almost like it was just the same tree repeated over and over again. She saw no sign of wildlife. Except for the occasional shadows that flitted by in the distance, and she didn't think those were animals.

If it were not for the faint marks of Minty's hooves, Nora would have had no clue which way to go.

"Hello? Minty? Here, Minty?" she called, unable to bear the silence any longer. But she received no response.

The pain in her leg only got worse as she limped on. She couldn't tell how long she'd been walking through the forest, but she felt exhausted.

Finally the distance started to brighten, and the air started to prickle. She slowed, rubbing her arms. The closer she grew to the light, the more the air tingled, reminding her of the magic in the swamp tree. She squinted, but she couldn't make out anything beyond the trees. Taking a shaky breath, she pushed forward and into the light.

She gasped.

Before her was a beautiful meadow, filled with hundreds of colorful flowers around a lake that shone like crystal, fed by a waterfall tumbling down from the mountain beyond it, filling the meadow with a soft mist. Around the lake and in the mist danced wispy figures, fading in and out of focus.

Except for the figure closest to her, a pale, rose-colored ethereal being, hovering slightly. It turned towards Nora and met her eyes.

Then, the vision vanished. Tangled, wilted grass replaced the flowers, and the water became murky, the waterfall a trickle. And instead of the dancing ghosts, there was only Minty.

"Minty!" Nora cried, dashing to the horse's side and throwing her arms about its neck. The mare nickered affectionately, bending its neck around Nora to return the hug.

Then Nora looked past her horse, and her eyes widened. A harpy stood there, in purple robes that swirled like smoke and a golden circlet on her head, smiling warmly.

"Andrea?" Nora released Minty.

The harpy opened her arms in greeting, her green eyes sparkling. "Nora."

Nora ran to embrace her friend. "What are you doing here?"

Andrea wrapped both her arms and feathered wings around

Nora. "The voices told me you'd be here, and that you'd need my help," Andrea said. As a harpy seer, she heard whispering voices that warned her of danger to come. "Though I almost doubted when I first saw this place, until your horse appeared. But why are you here? And where are your other friends?"

"We were separated," said Nora. "So much has happened since we left your valley." Looking over Andrea's shoulder she saw a second harpy. He was of the regular variety: No arms, bat-like wings, and taloned bird feet.

Andrea released Nora. "Have you at least been successful on your hunt for the riddles?"

"Yes, in part. We've found two of them and think we know where the third is hidden. But soldiers found us, so they might be hunting down Chris. And there's news of another war starting between the two Raecs."

"That is not surprising, though bad all the same," said Andrea. "The riddles were originally revealed in a time of war." She looked around the clearing. "But we shouldn't talk here. This is a dying, haunted place."

"Did you see it the way I did? As a beautiful glade?"

Andrea's brow furrowed, and she shook her head. "No. Did you see it that way when you first entered?"

"Yes. And I thought I saw a spirit…" Nora glanced around. "I felt— It looked so sad. This place is strange." She shivered.

"Indeed. If you wish, my friend and I can give you a lift. I don't think it would be safe for you to walk back through the forest. I will take you wherever you need to go."

A broad smile broke out across Nora's face. "Those words are music to my ears. I need to go east. As close to the Kaln as you can take me."

Once she reached the river, finding River's Cross would be easy.

❧

Christopher

Marc's hooves gave one final clop as they left the wooden bridge. Chris glanced back over his shoulder at the town. He'd left a note for Nora saying they had waited as long as they could. She would know where they were heading.

He turned forward again, to the south. It would take them at least a week to reach Dawncliff. And to get there, they would have to ride straight past the capital.

He took a deep breath, urging his horse into a trot. He felt relieved to get back on the hunt for King Miles's riddles. The magic dreams seemed to have stopped—the last one he'd heard was back in the swamp, when Terrin almost sleepwalked off the edge of the raft—but the widespread anger toward South Raec worried him. Whatever was waiting at the end of his quest, he knew the stakes were much higher than just proving his own innocence.

By alternating between trotting and walking, the group made good progress that morning. When the sun shone high overhead, Chris signaled his friends to a walk. Beads of sweat trickled into his eyes. Wiping his brow, he turned to face the others. "I say we stop for lunch here."

They nodded and dismounted.

Chris started to dismount, but paused. In the distance, a horseback rider was approaching at a canter.

"What is it?" asked Arnold, turning to follow Chris's gaze. His hand dropped to the hilt of his sword.

"It's fine," said Chris. "It's just one person. Most likely has nothing to do with us."

"No," said Terrin. "I think… it looks like Nora."

"Nora!" Arnold and Chris exclaimed together.

Arnold, Terrin, and Thomas climbed back into their saddles and turned their horses.

Chris had already signaled Marc to a canter. As he grew closer to the other rider, he recognized Nora's long, blond hair and the dappled coat of Minty.

Nora slowed to a walk when they were a few hundred feet away and waved. A broad smile split her face. "You're all alright," she said around pants for breath.

"We were the ones worried about you!" said Chris. "I'm sorry we didn't wait longer."

"No, no. You waited more than long enough."

"Nora! You're just in time for lunch," said Arnold, pulling to a stop beside Chris. Terrin and Thomas were close behind him. "Where's your saddle?"

"It's a long story," said Nora.

PART TWO

∾ 12 ∾

Arnold, 11 Years Earlier

Arnold scuffed his feet against the gravel path, absentmindedly twirling the two sticks he held.

"You seem out of it today," said Chris, walking behind him.

"I'd just forgotten how much of a pain school is," Arnold grumbled. He glanced around the school buildings, then turned to face Chris. "Hey, duel with me, will you?"

"I thought we were planning to study."

"Don't feel like it," said Arnold, holding out one stick to Chris. "Sword training's more important, anyway."

Chris sighed and accepted the stick.

"You always beat me," he said.

"That's not— Well, yeah, it's true. But you are improving. And you're better than anyone else here."

As the two boys moved off the path, the few students around them scattered. Those present the previous year had learned of

Arnold's joy for dueling, and they herded away the uninformed.

"You initiate," said Arnold.

He spun the branch around his wrist again, getting a feel for its weight. Chris flexed his wrist, but could not pull off the same trick. The two held still for a moment, then Chris lunged with a side swing. Arnold parried it, then jabbed Chris's stomach.

"How many times do I have to tell you, you're wide open," scolded Arnold as he stepped back and once again took a defensive stance.

Chris tightened his grip and started circling in slow, careful steps. Arnold turned with him, taking a step back. Chris danced forward and stabbed. Arnold sidestepped, sweeping his own stick under Chris's and stopping just short of his stomach.

"See? I'm no good at this," said Chris. "There's a reason I'm going to be a scholar, not a knight."

"You just need to work on your reflexes. Don't put so much force behind a swing that you can't change its direction. I'll go first this time. You're better at defense."

The boys stepped apart. Arnold twirled his branch again, taking a fencing stance. He rushed forward, swinging from his inside. Chris narrowly raised his stick to block it, staggering sideways.

Arnold pulled back his weapon and swung again, this time from the right. Once again, Chris barely blocked it.

Arnold continued to rain down a flurry of blows, pushing Chris back. Chris panted heavily, but stopped each one. One side swing he spun over his head, and lunged inward at Arnold, but Arnold dropped his sword to duck under the blow, and kicked out, sweeping Chris off his feet.

"Ow," said Chris, wincing in pain. "That was cheating."

"Sorry. I guess I got carried away," Arnold said picking up both their sticks. "Forgot it wasn't a real duel."

"Would you two stop it?"

Arnold turned to face the speaker, a young girl sitting beside the school fountain. He hadn't noticed how far they had moved during their duel.

The girl set the book she was holding in her lap and crossed her arms. "Shouldn't you be studying? This is a school, not a sparring arena."

"Well, excuse me, but I'm in training to be a knight. I'm only here because my mother insisted. Why do you even care what we do with our time?"

"I wouldn't, except I *am* trying to study. And you're interrupting."

"Then study somewhere else."

Chris grabbed Arnold's arm. "Arnold, don't," he hissed. "You shouldn't fight with her. She's the ambassador-in-training for the forest people of Xell."

"She's an ambassador?" Arnold said and burst into laughter. "Her? She's what? Six years old?"

The girl hopped to her feet, and Arnold was annoyed to see she stood an inch taller than him.

"Seven, obviously," she said. "But you know, forest people mature faster than you plains folk, so I'm more like… twenty-five."

"You spouted off a random number, didn't you?"

The girl rolled her eyes.

"Arnold, let's go," said Chris. "This is a pointless argument. And we need to study."

"Fine. I don't like wasting time with children, anyway." Arnold spun and stalked away towards the library.

"Children!" the girl exclaimed. "*You're* the one acting like a child."

Arnold waved his hand at her without turning back. "Yes, O

Great Ambassador. See if I come help you when you're attacked by a dragon, forest brat."

"Dragons aren't even real. And if they were, I could fight them just fine on my own. Probably better than you. What are you going to do when it takes off flying? I bet you can't hit the side of a castle with a bow and arrow."

Arnold spun back to face her. "Oh yeah? Well, I bet you're worse than Chris in a duel."

"Give me one of those sticks and we'll see."

"We *will* see!" Arnold chucked a stick at her as hard as he could.

She sidestepped to avoid being struck, but caught it. She took a fighting stance, spinning it around her fingers as he'd done earlier, smirking.

"Stop fighting," said Chris.

"I will when he apologizes."

"I will when she apologizes."

They paused, realizing they'd spoken at the same time, then glared at each other.

"What do I have to apologize for, exactly?" said the girl. "I merely stated a reasonable complaint as to your effect on my studying."

"Well, I was only stating a reasonable complaint as to your effect on my... ah..."

The girl rolled her eyes. "This is a complete waste of my time. Here, have your toy."

"Childr—" Arnold started, but the girl lunged forward and struck his leg. He yelped and fell to the ground. She swung again, stopping just short of his neck.

"That was cheating," said Arnold.

"I'm sorry, I thought you meant a real honest-to-goodness duel. In the forest that means no limits held. I figured such a great knight as yourself could manage a basic surprise attack." The girl dropped the stick, turned, grabbed her books from the fountain, and stalked away.

"Arnold, you should really apologize to Terrin," Chris said as he helped Arnold to his feet. "Forest people are proud, and you did insult her."

"Terrin, huh? Just you wait, Terrin. You'll regret this!" Arnold shouted after her.

Terrin mimicked his hand waving. "Oh, I'm so frightened. Much like those dragons you won't be slaying for me."

Arnold made a sound between a growl and a yell, and kicked the ground.

"Arnold—" Chris said.

"I can't believe my father's making me go to this stupid school, just because Mother wanted it."

"Arnold!" Chris gaped at him. "You shouldn't talk about your mother like that. She wanted you to have options besides knighthood, for a reason. She didn't want you locked into one thing. You should appreciate the opportun—"

"I don't care about my education! I want to be a knight, so I can protect people. School is just a useless delay."

೫ 13 ೫

Arnold

Arnold blinked his eyes as he slid into consciousness. He was surprised to see Terrin looking down at him, a frown etched in her sharp features.

"Is it my watch already? I thought I came after Chris," he mumbled.

"You looked like you were having a bad dream," she said.

"Oh. Yeah, I was. Kind of."

He sat up and stretched. Darkness blanketed the plains, the moon absent. But a million stars twinkled down, clear as diamonds.

"You know, I used to be sort of a jerk," Arnold said.

Terrin snorted. "Don't I know it. But then, I wasn't the nicest person either."

"I think I've come further than you," he teased.

She jabbed his side. "Don't be rude. Though you're right. You've changed a lot. Neither of us were very happy people then."

"And now we're the best of friends," he said, waving his hand in time with his sing-songy voice. "Adventuring across the country.

Neither of us doing what we'd planned, but happy all the same."

Terrin rolled her eyes.

He grinned at her. "That's something that hasn't changed since the start. I think you must have some sort of 'constantly rolling eyes' disease."

"Yes, it's an allergic reaction to idiot knights," said Terrin. "But on a serious note, are you sure you're happy, following Chris? You had a dream, a good one. And now, instead of serving your country, you might be charged with treason by your own king."

"I think we had this conversation when we first left Fredricburg. My answer is the same. If anything, I'm more confident in this choice. Protecting my best friend, my three best friends, is the most important thing I could be doing right now."

Terrin smiled. "Then I guess we're both sure. I didn't really doubt it, but… What would we do without you to keep us cheerful?" She shoved at his shoulder as she stood up. "Anyway, you should get back to sleep, and I'm supposed to be keeping watch. Good night."

"Good night."

≈

Arnold blinked, surprised to find himself surrounded by hundreds of people. No, not surrounded, he floated above them. He took a moment to recognize that he was in Coricstead. He'd only been there once, but he had seen little of the city. His father had kept him close at all times.

He turned, wondering why he was here now, and why—*how*—he was floating. *Obviously it's a dream,* he pointed out to himself.

He glided through the streets. Beneath him, people chattered and yelled, carts rattled, boots tapped, but the sounds were distant, as through a bubble. The faces, too, seemed blurry, as if he couldn't focus on the details. After several minutes, he found himself in the town square. A large courtyard surrounding a statue of King Miles, founder of the Coric dynasty. From every side, merchants hawked their wares to the hundreds of people that struggled to maneuver around each other.

He turned in place for a moment, then saw a bulletin board. It seemed sharper than the other features of the dream, so he approached it. Announcements, old and new, hung from it, including several wanted posters. His gaze searched over them, expecting to see Chris's face, at least. Probably the rest of the group as well.

But they weren't there. He checked again, just to be sure.

Arnold turned away, wondering where to go next. A flicker of movement caught his attention. He spun to see a man, dressed in a ratty cloak with its hood pulled over his head, pushing his way through the crowd.

Following close behind, Arnold glided over the people. Though he could only see a hood, the man seemed more in focus than everything else. Even his footsteps sounded clearer.

The man went a few blocks before turning into a busy inn. Arnold slipped through the door just behind him.

Tenants crowded the inn's bar room. Cups clattered, men guffawed, a band played with debatable skill. But to Arnold the entire pub sounded like it was underwater. The cloaked man went straight to a table in the back corner, shrouded by thick shadows. He pulled back a chair, the scrape of its legs against the floor deafening compared to everything else.

A maid made her round to his table, but the hooded figure requested only a glass of water.

Out of the shadows, another figure leaned forward. Arnold

jerked back. He'd not seen this man sitting there. On a closer look, he recognized Duke Grith. He'd never imagined the duke coming to a scroungy bar like this.

"What have you to report?" said the duke.

"They're just outside the city now, headed to Dawncliff."

Arnold couldn't place the low, rasping voice, though it sounded familiar, but he knew that the man meant himself, Chris, and the others.

But we're still a day or two away from Coricstead. Arnold thought. *And how does he know we're going to Dawncliff?*

"They're hoping to find the next riddle there," the hooded man continued. "Christopher seems to be the only one capable of reading the writing."

"And?" The duke's fingers drummed against the table. "None of this is important enough for you to have needed to meet with me. In case you haven't realized, I'm an influential man who can't just run off whenever I want, without it being noticed. My time is valuable."

The hooded figure dropped his head. His voice trembled when he next spoke.

"I know. I needed to reach you for something else. The charm you gave me, it's been on the fritz for a while now."

The figure pulled a necklace from his pocket. A dull white stone hung from it, circled by an assortment of silver animals. Arnold recognized a hawk, a rabbit, a mouse, and a deer before the duke's hand closed around the pendant.

He held it in his palm for a moment, rubbing his thumb against it in slow circles.

"It seems most of the magic has been sucked out of it." The duke frowned. "An easy fix, but how much have you been using it?"

"Maybe five shifts."

"That shouldn't have come even close to draining it." The duke's frown deepened, and then he smiled. "How very interesting. I wonder…"

The duke shut his eyes, and for the next few minutes nothing seemed to happen. Then the stone began to glow, taking on a bluish hue. The cloaked figure straightened.

The duke's eyes opened, then widened. He turned, searching the room. His gaze settled on Arnold. The duke raised his free hand, and for a second, pain lanced through Arnold's body. Then his surrounding warped, and he was being pulled back away.

As he jerked to consciousness, the pain ceased. He panted for breath, staring up at the stars without seeing them.

What was that? Arnold wondered. Was it one of the vision-dreams like Chris had, back when they started their quest? But who was the hooded man? How had he known their plans? Or that only Chris could read the riddles?

He rolled over. He could see Chris on watch, but he remained silent. Chris had enough to worry about. Arnold would wait for a better time, and for proof that the dream was true.

❧ 14 ❧

Brayden

The wind was strong, pressing the grass flat. Above the group of twenty or so nobles, a circling hawk shrieked. The group watched it, and, as it dove towards some brush, they turned their horses to follow, King Orin at the head.

Gillian had argued against Brayden joining the hawking party, and Brayden had not been thrilled himself. He didn't get along with birds, no matter how hard he tried. The few times he'd gone hawking had not ended well for him.

But he hardly wanted to turn down an invitation from the king himself.

He'd borrowed a peregrine from the royal mews, but had not yet been asked to release it to hunt. He could imagine that, under its hood, the bird had an angry glint in its eye as it plotted how to make a fool of him in front of the king.

Baron Torc, whose bird they'd just been following, called his hawk back to his arm, giving it a chunk of meat. A squire ran to collect the hare it had slain.

"Prince Brayden, your falcon has not yet wet its claws," said the king. "Perhaps we should give it a fly."

Brayden's throat went dry, but he bowed his head. "I'd be honored."

He started to untie the leather cord binding the bird's hood, but paused when Baron Torc said, "Who's that?"

The entire party turned to look. A rider was galloping towards them. He stopped just short of the party, the messenger's regalia clear on his saddle blanket and armband.

"Is there a Prince Brayden Coric here?" the messenger asked.

"That's me," said Brayden, urging his horse forward.

The man bowed deeply in the saddle. "The ambassador Gillian Fredrico has sent me to summon you at once. He says it's very urgent."

Brayden's initial reaction was of irritation. Was Gillian so determined to keep him from embarrassing himself that he'd make this sort of scene?

No, Gillian was not that bad of an ambassador. Perhaps this *was* important.

Brayden turned to face King Orin and bowed his head again. "I hate to leave in the middle of a hunt. But if I may beg your permission—"

"Of course," the king said, returning the bow. "I hope it is nothing too serious."

❦

Brayden burst through the door into the North Raecan ambassadorial house. His toe caught on the threshold, and he hopped several times to keep from falling.

As he straightened, he saw Gillian waiting for him at the end of the hall, arms crossed. The ambassador didn't react to Brayden's fumble, but spoke immediately.

"I hope you've enjoyed your stay, but you have been recalled to North Raec by the king, your father."

"Already?" said Brayden. "Your request couldn't have reached him that quickly."

"Perhaps not, but these came today."

He unfolded his arms to hold out two letters.

Brayden shut the door and took them. The first was addressed to Gillian. It stated briefly that Brayden was to return to North Raec, and that it was in Gillian's hands to make the preparations as soon as possible.

The second, unopened letter was addressed for Brayden's eyes only.

"I've already sent a servant to the wharf to find and book passage on the next suitable ship leaving for Coricstead. Would you like to send your regrets to King Orin yourself, or should I handle that as well?" Gillian asked, a smug smile splitting his face.

"I think that I'd like to read my own letter before I do anything rash. I'll be in my room if you need me, but take no more actions without my permission."

He strode past Gillian to the stairs.

"Don't trip on your way up," was all Gillian said.

In his room, Brayden shut the door and sat cross-legged on his bed. Taking a deep breath, he broke the seal on the letter and pulled out a sheet of paper. He unfolded it and gently smoothed the creases. He recognized the cramped handwriting, accented by giant loops, to indeed be his father's.

> *Brayden,*
> *I hope this finds you in good health, and that the task you were given has gone well.*

You will recall the theft of one of the Riddled Stone Shards earlier this spring, by the young Christopher Fredrico. At the time, we considered the matter of minor importance, but since you left, the Shard from Tamburg has disappeared as well.

In light of the threat from South Raec, I have re-evaluated these thefts to be a serious danger. I'm sure you understand why we can't explain the significance of this to anyone outside the family. Please inform the ambassador that it is a private matter.

I've already asked him to arrange your immediate departure, and he will handle any political consequences.

The letter was signed with his father's seal.

Brayden refolded the paper, slid it into the envelope, and leaned back against the bedstead. He understood why his father would find the theft of a second Shard concerning, though he wasn't quite sure why he needed to return home.

Perhaps Tyler had used the situation as leverage to convince their father that Brayden wasn't safe.

Of course, Tyler was right. In coming to South Raec, Brayden had nearly died. But what did that have to do with the Shards? The people outside the royal family who knew the real value of the Shards could be counted on two hands. They were all people the king would trust with his life. There was no way the South Raecans knew.

And, so far, he had no evidence that anyone here had sent the assassin. Not even a gut feeling.

The thought that had been nagging at the back of his mind now came to the forefront. Perhaps it was not a South, but a North Raecan who had tried to kill him.

Either way, he could no longer make Gillian let him stay. He would return to North Raec.

He could only hope that his sudden departure did not offend King Orin.

§

Nora

Nora, Chris, Terrin, and Arnold lounged at the edge of a small woods that marked the boundary between two fenced pastures. In the distance, Nora could see Coricstead, but the friends had stayed clear of the main road where someone might see them.

"There he is," said Chris.

Nora could make out several travelers spaced along the road, some on foot, some with wagons, some alone, and some in groups. Most were headed for the capital, but one particular horseback rider was coming away from the city and had turned off the road to ride for the trees.

When Thomas drew near, she was pleased to see a new saddle for her tied behind his own. Thomas dismounted and started untying it.

"How did it go?" asked Chris.

"For starters," the old man said, "what funds we had are now mostly depleted. But I doubt we'll have much use for money from here out."

"Why?" said Arnold. "Were there wanted posters for us?"

"Several," said Thomas. He undid the last knot and slid Nora's new saddle from its spot, handing it to her. "And judging from the numbers in the city, I would think that it won't be long before your faces are spread through the country. I recommend that we avoid other travelers as much as possible."

Chris sighed. "I guess they were North Raecan soldiers after all," he muttered under his breath. Nora wasn't sure what he meant, and no one else seemed to notice the comment.

Terrin and Thomas were both looking at Arnold, whose eyes had glazed over. He stared down the hill contemplatively.

Still watching Arnold, Thomas pulled something from his saddlebag. "Here, I got this for you."

"Ah." Arnold's head snapped around. He blinked a couple times. "What is it?" he asked, taking the device from Thomas.

"A prosthetic. It can't replace your hand, but it will let you use that shield of yours again."

"Neat," Arnold said, without enthusiasm. He turned the device in his good hand, and the metal fingers clicked against each other.

"Arnold?" said Chris. "Is something wrong?"

"Nah… Just mourning that we'll never sleep in a proper bed again."

"Don't be so melodramatic," said Terrin, rolling her eyes. "Look at it this way: you also won't have to sleep in another hammock."

He rubbed his chin for a second, then nodded. "That seems like a fair trade."

Nora laughed. Arnold had discovered during their stay with the forest people that he and hammocks did not get along.

Chris stood and stretched his legs. "Well, if we are that famous around here, we should try to put some distance between us and the capital before nightfall. And it'll give Nora a chance to break in the new saddle."

ᚙ 15 ᚙ

Brayden

Coughs wracked through Brayden's body, spewing brackish water from his mouth. His fingers dug into the grass and earth. When the fit passed, he collapsed sideways, trembling with cold. Every breath was fire in his chest, but he was glad to be breathing.

"I found the kid prince!" hollered someone nearby.

Brayden turned slightly to see the thick frame of a sailor standing over him.

A sadistic grin split the man's face. "Don't you look like a drowned rat?"

"Only half drowned," Brayden rasped. He regretted it as another series of coughs started.

The man guffawed.

Over his coughing, Brayden could hear that someone had yelled a response, but couldn't make out the words. He was surprised when the man's arms closed around him. His mind was heavy with fog, and for a second he tried to struggle. He could barely convince his finger to twitch.

As the man moved, the air became warmer. By the time the man set him down, his face felt like it was a step away from being burned off. He could make out the flickering of flames.

"Here's one soaking wet, useless prince, as requested," said the sailor. "Always funny when the landlubbers take a swim."

"We should be glad he's alive," grumbled another voice. Brayden recognized this one as belonging to the ship's captain. "I've seen plenty of tested and true seamen come out of a storm looking worse than that. Go back to where you found him. If he washed up, then there's a good chance some of the ship's store is there, too."

When the captain spoke again a second later, he was no longer across the fire, but instead knelt beside him. "Here, boy. Have some water."

A strong arm propped him up, holding the water skin to his mouth and allowing just a splash of liquid through. Brayden swallowed it. Against his still-burning chest, it felt like ice. Good ice.

After three mouthfuls, the captain laid him back down. "I'm going to help the crew search. You should be out of danger now, so rest."

Now that his mind was clearing, Brayden wanted to rise and help, but his limbs felt like anchors.

A few days had passed since he had received the letter from his father ordering him back to North Raec. He had given his apologies to King Orin who, despite the vague nature of Brayden's 'family issue,' had said that he understood, repeated his hope that it was nothing too serious, and asked Brayden to convey the proposal for a new treaty directly to his father.

Gillian had found a North Raecan cargo ship bound for

Coricstead leaving the next day. The captain had not been happy to take on living cargo at the last minute, but he'd been well compensated, and he couldn't exactly say no to his own prince. The ship's crew had mostly ignored him, except when they ordered him to get his cursed highness out of the way.

During the storm, they had sent him below, to the captain's cabin. He remembered water flooding in, and desperate shouts from the crew. The ship tossing beneath him. Then the floor itself had seemed to slide away. He'd struck his head on something, and the next thing he knew, he was underwater. It was luck and adrenaline that had let him swim to shore, though he'd swallowed what felt like gallons of sea water on the way.

At least he was alive. But he was frustrated that now, when the crew couldn't have stopped him from helping, his body stopped him instead.

Reluctantly, he shut his eyes and let his mind glide away to unconsciousness.

☙

Waking up felt like he was back in the water, swimming for all he was worth but unable to tell which way was up or down or forward or back, with currents pushing and pulling him whichever way he didn't want to go.

Through the fog, Brayden could hear voices coming into focus, letting him catch snatches and snippets of conversation.

"Slept like a log."

"Useless brat."

"Lucky to survive."

"Better wake up soon."

He groaned, trying to push himself away from the ground.

"Still a bit water-logged, huh?"

He opened his eyes to see the captain leaning towards him. "I was worried you wouldn't wake up, boy. Come on, breakfast's ready. Even worse than what we had on board, but at least it's warm."

The captain stood and disappeared from Brayden's sight. With another groan, the prince rolled himself over and dragged his body to its feet.

The ship's crew had gathered in a rough circle several yards away. Few of the men were unscathed, but the group seemed no smaller than before. The captain himself—a short but well-muscled man—had developed a slight limp.

The seamen cast glares at him as he approached.

He took a small portion of slightly warmed hardtack and jerky. It tasted like sea water, but when washed down with a few mouthfuls of fresh water, it made for a filling breakfast.

The captain plopped down beside him as he was finishing the small meal. "Well, Prince Brayden," he said, "I'm afraid my transportation was perhaps not as satisfying as you'd hoped for. We were lucky to wash up safely, though, if a bit far from civilization."

Brayden wanted to tell him it wasn't his fault, but the man continued quickly.

"I'd say we're east of the Kaln. Since we're out of a boat, your best bet would be to head west, find a town, and get another boat headed north. We'll be headed for the nearest riverside town ourselves, so we might as well stick together that far. But you're alone from there. We haven't the money to go all the way back to Coricstead."

Brayden shook his head. "I'm not sure I have the money, either, and I doubt anyone would take my word for it that I am a prince."

"Well, some of your things washed up over there." The captain pointed. "Not much, but you might have something."

Brayden found a few piles of cargo they'd scavenged from the wreck, and a pile of ship parts. A small bag and his dagger comprised his personal salvage. His main travel pack was not to be seen.

His bag was ruined, and none of the remaining items were of value.

With a sigh, he tossed the bag away and considered his options. Without a way to secure passage from commoners, he'd have to go cross-country on foot. If he could find a main road, it wouldn't be too bad, but traveling alone in this part of North Raec was ill-advised.

And food would be another problem altogether.

He tied his knife to his belt and turned to find the captain. "I have a proposition that I hope will be beneficial to both of us."

"Oh?" said the captain, arching his left eyebrow but not even looking at Brayden.

"If I'm correct, you won't be able to scrape enough together from selling this wreckage to buy another ship. And if you do have enough money saved up somewhere, you'll have to get there first, and you'll lose most of your crew before then."

"Maybe." The captain still didn't look at him.

"I'd like to hire you and your crew to accompany me across country to Coricstead."

The captain turned to face him. He leaned on his elbow, bearded chin against his fist, giving his voice a garbled sound. "If you don't have money to buy your way up the river, how are you going to pay us?"

"With my name. When we arrive, I'll request that my father, the king, reward you with a new ship, a better ship, and pay for the journey."

"You seem like an honest kid, if nothing else," said the Captain.

"But how can I be sure your father will be so interested in paying up?"

"I give you my word as a Coric, and as your prince. My father will honor that word."

The captain mulled it over, then nodded. "All right. I can't guarantee my full crew will risk the venture, but I've known several of these men half my life. You'll have your bodyguard."

"Thank you," said Brayden. "Oh, and I'd appreciate if you and your men don't let on that I'm the prince until we reach Coricstead. And that you treat me as one of the crew."

The captain laughed. "I'm not sure you'll fit in. But I'll tell them."

❧ 16 ❧

Nora

Nora watched as Thomas helped Arnold adjust the straps of his prosthetic. It was a sleeve of flexible metal that reminded her of the armored gloves many knights wore. It could be tightened or loosened around the forearm with leather straps, with two extra straps anchoring it to the upper arm. The fingers were ratcheted, allowing them to be bent different degrees and then locked into position.

Nora had never seen such a useful device. She had, in fact, only seen one prosthetic before. A Yorc of her mountain village had had his arm crushed in a landslide. He sometimes wore a wooden arm that strapped around his shoulder. Unlike this, it did little to replace his arm, but was more for looks.

"It feels weird," said Arnold, flexing his arm. "I hadn't realized just how much I'd adjusted to not having a hand, until I put this on."

"If you give it time, you'll get used to it," said Thomas. "Do you want to try holding your shield?"

Arnold grabbed the shield from its position next to his pack. Nora hadn't seen him use it since the harpy attack. When they faced the wolves, there had been no time, and once he lost his hand…

It was a simple, round shield, covered in white cloth. Underneath the cloth, it bore the symbol of a King's Knight, one who had not yet received the honor of his own coat-of-arms. Since the group had gone rogue, Arnold had kept the emblem hidden.

He slid the shield over his arm, but as he went to tighten his new hand around the handle, his real fingers stroked the shield's edge. He smiled weakly and then bent his fingers into place.

When he had secured the shield, he stood and turned his arm this way and that.

"Is that better?" asked Thomas.

"Yeah," said Arnold. "I guess."

Nora clambered to her feet and jogged to her bag, pulling out the simple mock blade he had carved for her. "Arnold, duel me."

"What? You only last two seconds when I don't have the shield. Do you think—"

"Not for my training, silly," said Nora. "So you can get used to the hand."

"Oh. Sure." Arnold bent to find his own practice blade.

"Get him, Nora," Terrin cheered from where she and Chris sat, enjoying a cup of tea.

Nora threw Terrin a smile. "You know me, I always give 110 percent. No one can stand against me, and all that."

Terrin laughed.

The thought crossed Nora's mind that Terrin might not be so cheerful if she knew about Nora's adventure in the Dark Forest. She'd meant to tell them, but thinking of what Terrin had been through, she'd decided against it. She didn't have a clue how to interpret what she'd seen there, but she was sure there had been at least one spirit involved. So she had left the story at being lost in the woods, Minty getting spooked so that Nora lost her saddle, and then racing to catch up with the others.

She sighed inwardly as she flexed the sword in her hand and dropped into a sideways fencing stance, her eyes locking on Arnold's.

"Ready?" she asked.

"Ready."

She leaped forward, even as he finished the 'dy', and jabbed him with a quick thrust.

His eyes seemed to clear as she moved. He twisted, knocking her sword away with his shield. The blow threw her off balance, but she spun with the momentum, dancing away from him as she did so.

He returned her thrust, his blade aiming straight for her chest. She barely deflected it to clip her shoulder.

She winced, but moved forward towards him. Too late, she realized that his shield covered most of her striking area. She twisted her wrist to strike beneath the shield. He dropped the shield to block her blow, then angled the shield up, pushing her sword back into her with all his strength.

She pulled her sword off the shield, only to feel the shield itself ram into her body, throwing her backwards. She squeaked with pain as she landed.

"Fighting against a shield is a whole different classroom, isn't it?" said Arnold. He took a step back.

Nora's eyes shut, blue blurring their edges. Her lungs throbbed, not from heavy breathing but from the anger that clawed against them.

She frowned. On one hand she could count the times she'd

been angry in her life, but the outbursts that resulted from that anger tended to be huge. There was no need for that now.

Taking a deep breath, she forced out a laugh as she clambered to her feet.

"So much for nothing standing against me," she said.

"Well, you know what they say," said Arnold. "There's always a bigger dragon."

This time Nora's laugh was genuine, and the anger vanished as swiftly as it had appeared.

"Again?" Arnold asked.

Nora hesitated for a moment, then nodded.

ॐ

Brayden

As he dunked the water skin into the bucket, the cold water splashed over Brayden's hand. He almost pulled back, but he forced himself to wait until the bubbles pouring from the skin's mouth stopped, showing it to be full.

He lifted it, and water poured off the sides. Screwing on the cap, he stepped back to let the next man fill his skin.

The previous day, they had carried what they could scavenge from the ship to a nearby town to trade for food. Their supplies were still short. The captain had dispersed what they had among his men, twenty of whom stayed to look for work where they were. Ten remained, besides Brayden and the captain. Some out of loyalty, but most just felt they'd have better luck job hunting in the capital.

Now it was late afternoon of the following day. They'd paused in this little hamlet to take advantage of its well, since the nearest stream was a couple miles out of their way.

Brayden turned away from the well and went to where the captain and a few other sailors waited. The captain had been right about him not fitting in. He stopped at the edge of their group, but the sailors still shifted away from him. Though he was as tall, if not taller, than most of them, his build was lanky, whereas they were thick. Even the short captain looked like he could snap Brayden's arm.

Reynard, the captain's son, had been the most vocal about his distrust of Brayden, or at least of Brayden's father. "What does a stuck-up prince and his father care for peasants like us? What reason will they have for keeping their word? None. They'll take our help and give us no reward."

The captain had asked forgiveness for his son's rash words, but Brayden didn't mind them. But he feared the consequences if that sort of opinion spread through the entire country. People looking down on him, he was used to. People looking down on his father or brother, though—

He sighed.

"Time to head off," said the captain, rousing Brayden from his thoughts.

As they trooped out of the village, Reynard leaned over and whispered, "The well water not to your royal fancy?"

Brayden ignored him, quickening his pace.

❧ 17 ❧

Brayden

The air was temperate, even chilly as night grew closer, but sweat still beaded on Brayden's temple. His body ached from days of marching and sleeping on the ground. The previous night, they'd begged the use of an innkeeper's empty barn—after the whole village showed up to hear stories of their travels—but hay was little better than grass.

The group trekked single file along the rutted road, Brayden near the middle. To their left rose a hill of boulders, dotted with scraggly bushes. To their right stretched the moor scattered with tors and the occasional tree, silhouetted dauntingly against the evening sky.

"Boo!" breathed a voice behind him.

Brayden half jumped out of his crawling skin and spun to face the voice, his hand closing around the hilt of his knife. It was only Douglas, the ship's cook, one of the two men behind him.

"You should have seen the look on your face." Douglas chuckled, but Brayden just shrugged and trudged on.

But—

There should have been six men behind him.

He spun back around. The shadowy, bearded figure behind the cook was raising a knife. Brayden shouted, grabbing Douglas and pulling him away. They staggered and fell. The blade swung, just missing the cook but cutting his shirt.

Brayden hit the ground, the bigger man landing on top and crushing him.

Douglas rolled off Brayden, froze as he saw the armed man, then started scrambling backwards. "Bandits! Bandits!" he screamed.

Chest throbbing, Brayden looked past the bandit. He could see the limp bodies of the other sailors, and three more bandits rising from the side of the road.

The bearded bandit stepped past Brayden toward the cook, his long knife poised to strike. Farther down the road, the crewmen had turned back, but the closest man was several yards away. The blade swung down.

Brayden rolled and lunged forward.

He grabbed the bandit's leg and jerked it sideways. The bandit yelped and tumbled backwards, his arms flailing and knife swinging wide.

Leaping to his feet, Douglas pulled out his blade. The other sailors drew their own swords and knives as they ran.

The fallen bandit thrashed backwards, now fleeing from his prey. Brayden winced as the bandit's heels connected with his side. He rolled away before pulling himself to his feet.

He drew his dagger, but the captain put a hand on his arm. "We'll take care of this," he said. "Get out of here."

"Wait," said a burly bandit, stepping forward to help the first one up. "If you hand over the prince, no one else will get hurt."

Brayden's heart skipped a beat. How did these bandits know his identity?

A few sailors glanced back at him, no doubt considering the idea.

Then Reynard charged the speaker. The bandit blocked the first swing, but the blow threw him backwards. A second blow broke through the bandit's defenses, and he fell to the ground. He didn't move.

The bearded bandit scuttled away, almost falling again.

"No one was supposed to get hurt," Reynard roared, and lunged.

The captain echoed Reynard's roar, and the sailors all charged.

Brayden started after them, but a large, gloved fist closed around his arm and folded it across his body in a bear hug, yanking him back, while another hand covered his mouth. "No you don't, princey boy," snarled a voice behind his ear.

More bandits rushed past him towards the sailor's backs.

He did his best to scream through the gloves. The sound had no effect, and he couldn't bite down through the thick leather. He kicked his heel against his captor's shin. The man yelped. He did not release Brayden, but the captain and the cook turned to face the new attackers.

Brayden jerked back and forth as he struggled to free himself. But the man's grip only tightened.

"Hold still, you brat."

Brayden gritted his teeth, then let his body go limp. The man relaxed and lowered his hand from the boy's mouth to take away his dagger. At once, Brayden bunched all his muscles and threw himself forward, spinning away from the man. Then he kicked his captor as hard as he could. The man gasped, releasing his arm, and Brayden staggered backwards.

The man drew a deep breath, then drew his sword. "You'll pay, boy."

Brayden lunged, hoping to strike first. But the big man was fast, and Brayden barely blocked the first swing with his dagger. The sheer strength of the blow sent tremors through his body. He jumped back, adjusting his stance.

The bandit lunged. Instead of blocking, Brayden ducked beneath the blow, then surged up, knocking the bandit backwards. Taking a step forward, he pinned the man's sword arm beneath his boot, bending to wrench the sword free, while keeping his dagger towards the man.

The sword was heavy, but as Brayden stepped back, he kept both blades pointed at the bandit. "Get out of here."

"What, the prince doesn't even know how to kill?" the man snarled, pulling himself to his feet. "What has the royal family come to?" He took a slow step backwards.

A heavy boot struck Brayden's lower back, throwing him forward. As he fell, he tossed the knife aside and twisted, grabbing the sword with both hands to slash at this new attacker.

It was the bearded bandit. He staggered back, screaming and clutching his stomach. He fell, but was caught as another sword thrust through his chest from behind.

Reynard stepped past, throwing the dead bandit to the side. Reynard's clothes were torn, and blood drizzled from a cut on his forehead into his eye. But he wiped away the blood, raising his sword towards the big man.

"You," Reynard said.

"What?" the big man snarled, crouching to retrieve Brayden's dagger.

"This wasn't the deal."

"The deal?" The man laughed. "You treated with bandits, boy.

What did you expect?"

"Those were good men you killed." Reynard's voice trembled.

"Oh, I'm sorry. Did your wee, little friends get a bit sliced up? I didn't think you'd mind, considering how willingly you handed over your own prince to be ransomed."

Reynard screamed, lunging for the bandit with a downward swing.

"No!" cried Brayden, realizing Reynard's mistake.

The bandit sidestepped the attack. His dagger flashed once. Reynard stumbled and fell.

Brayden rolled to his feet and stepped between them, hefting the bandit's sword to strike. Even holding it with both hands, the blade was too heavy for him. The bandit stepped inside the blow and swung the hilt of the knife towards Brayden's head. He ducked and threw himself against the man's knees.

The bandit's leg buckled, but he took a step and caught himself. He grabbed Brayden's collar and tossed him sideways.

Brayden hit the ground hard, losing his hold on the sword. The bandit kicked him twice in the stomach. Brayden curled, fighting the tears that sprung to his eyes, coughing into the dust.

The man bent to grab his sword, sliding the dagger into his belt. He took one glance at where Reynard lay, then turned away.

Groaning, Brayden rolled over and tried to drag himself to his feet. Pain stabbed his chest, and he collapsed.

Down the path, the fighting was almost over. Only the cook and half the bandits were still standing. Douglas was already backing away from the bandits. He took a last glance at Reynard and Brayden. "I surrender," he cried as he turned and ran.

"Let him go," said the big man who had downed Reynard. "We've got our prize."

"He better be worth it," snapped another bandit. "We lost a lot of good fighters tonight. For one brat."

The chief bandit strode back towards Brayden.

He tried again to rise, but the man reached him before he could and kicked him again.

Brayden fell back, coughing. His vision blurred.

A battle cry rang across the moor.

ॐ 18 ॐ

Arnold

Even as Arnold shouted and signaled Rich with a nudge of his heel, he was slipping his shield from his back and over his arm. They burst from the trees and down the slope at a canter.

He could see lumps on the ground—almost a dozen bodies—and one man fleeing the scene. A handful of ragged-looking men watched him go, sheathing their swords. The biggest of the bandits stood several feet closer than the main group, leaning over a fallen body. He looked up at Arnold's cry and moved back. A rope dangled from his hands.

Arnold tilted his arm up to keep the shield from falling as one by one he bent the fingers into place. The distance between him and the big man narrowed. He had two fingers left to go and no time. Without drawing his sword, he bumped his knee against Rich's side. The horse veered to the right, and Arnold swung his shield at the man. The bandit jumped backwards, but not fast enough. The bottom of the shield clipped his chin, throwing him to the ground.

Arnold sat back, and Rich ground to a halt. A quick squeeze of his foot made the horse pivot to face the other bandits. They were leaping aside to avoid Chris, who had cantered down the slope at Arnold's heels.

Blood boiling at the sight of the bodies, Arnold drew his sword. Rich lunged towards the nearest bandit. With one swing, the man fell, gargling out a scream.

"Behind you!" shouted Terrin from atop the hill.

Arnold spun Rich to see that the first man had clambered back to his feet. He charged, ready to skewer the man, but the bandit slipped out of reach. Rich pivoted to face the man again and reared, his hooves thrashing.

The bandit leaped back, across the body he'd been standing over. A woman, or a youth? Arnold couldn't tell for sure. The man pointed his sword at the still form. "Make one move, and I end this one's life."

Arnold lowered his sword.

There was a whistle-thud, and the bandit's eyes went wide. He tumbled sideways, an arrow sticking from his back.

Arnold waved to Terrin, who stood at the top of the hill, bow raised. He didn't wait for a response, but turned Rich to see how Chris was doing.

He had dismounted and was going from body to body, checking for life.

"Did you get them?" asked Arnold, trotting over.

"No, they ran away. Sorry," he added, glancing up at Arnold.

Arnold's grip on his sword tightened. He stood in the saddle, to see if he could make out where the dastards had gone.

"I know how you feel about bandits," said Chris. "But don't go after them. It's not worth it."

Arnold gritted his teeth, then wiped and sheathed his sword.

"This boy's alive," called Nora.

Arnold turned back to see Nora crouched over the boy that the bandit had threatened. Thomas rose from beside another body and went to join Nora.

"Seems to be the only one," Chris said. He sighed.

Arnold jumped down from Rich's back. "How is he?"

"Unconscious," said Thomas. "But he doesn't appear to be bleeding anywhere."

"Is it safe to move him?" asked Chris.

"It should be," said Thomas. "It'll be hard to treat him here, anyway."

"Arnold?" asked Chris.

Arnold stepped forward, then remembered he still had his shield. "One second."

Opening the fingers was thankfully easier than shutting them had been. He pressed them a certain way, and they sprung straight. He slid the shield from his arm and over his back.

Then he bent and collected the boy in his arms. The kid was tall and lanky. Arnold guessed him to be no older than the farm boy, Michael. His brows were drawn together—from pain no doubt—but he showed no other response.

☙

"I've done all I can for him," said Thomas. He accepted a blanket from Nora and tucked it around the boy. "We'll have to wait till he wakes up. I don't think he has any head injuries, so it shouldn't be too long."

They'd moved camp from the cluster of trees on the other side of the hill. Arnold felt more exposed on top of the tor, but the healer had insisted because an outcropping of granite made it safe to kindle a fire. So now Arnold stared into the flames, his knees curled to his chest and arms crossed atop them. He'd removed his prosthetic and dropped the uncomfortable thing on the ground beside him.

"We should have been there sooner," he grumbled.

"We got there as fast as we could," said Chris, setting a hand on his shoulder.

"If we'd left our horses—"

"If we'd left our horses, they might have outmatched us," said Chris. "You're the only one here who's more than decent with a sword."

They had just settled down to sleep when the shouting had started. It had been faint, and only Arnold—who'd taken first watch—had heard it. Fortunately, the others hadn't been asleep yet, but it had still taken a few minutes for Chris and Arnold to saddle up. The others had gone on foot, since Terrin couldn't shoot as well from horseback, and Chris had vetoed Nora and Thomas getting involved in a fight, if they could help it.

"Arnold, why don't you rest? I'll take first watch for you," said Chris.

"I'm fine," Arnold grumbled. "Couldn't sleep if I wanted to."

"All right." Chris sighed. "Thomas, can you and Nora take turns watching the patient?"

"Of course," said Thomas, nodding. "I'll wake you in a couple hours, Nora."

Terrin, Chris, and Nora crawled into their bedrolls. Arnold dragged himself to his feet, and paced the edge of the tor, scuffing his feet as he went.

Thomas pulled out a bundle of bandages, unfolded them, and then started folding them again, humming softly.

಄

Terrin

It was hard for Terrin to sleep when she could feel Arnold's irritation radiating off of him as he paced. It seemed to permeate the air.

The thought of all those dead men, only a few hundred yards from them, didn't help. She rolled over, trying to ease the knot in her stomach.

It must be worse for Arnold, she thought. *Seeing that carnage must remind him of his mother.*

She remembered Chris explaining to her about Arnold's family, way back when they were kids. Arnold had always looked up to his father Sir Fredrico, Chris's uncle—a famous knight who'd given lessons to the king himself. But he'd been closer to his mother. She had always insisted on Arnold being gentle with animals, and on his giving school education a try, while his father had been bent on making him a knight.

Then, only a few months before Terrin had met Arnold for the first time, his mother had been traveling when bandits attacked. They killed her and most of the group with her. The few survivors had almost perished from exposure before some merchants found them.

After that, Arnold's father had softened to his wife's wishes for Arnold, but Arnold had changed his mind completely. He wanted nothing more than to hunt down the bandits that had killed his mother, and every other outlaw in North Raec while he was at it.

She sighed, twisting in her bedroll. *I'm sorry, Arnold. I wish I could help, but I don't know how.*

❧ 19 ❧

Christopher

The sky was graying when Nora shook Chris awake. He sat up, yawning. "What is it? I already took my watch," he asked, trying to comb through his thick, black hair with his hand. He soon gave up.

"Brayden's awake," Nora said, moving away from Chris, to where Arnold slept.

Chris blinked, trying to figure out who Brayden was. Then his eyes flew open as he remembered the previous evening's events. He struggled out of his blankets, turning towards the boy.

The kid was sitting up, his legs crossed, chatting with Thomas. Terrin paced the edges of their camp, on patrol, her gaze flickering between them and the surrounding moor. For a moment the boy met Chris's eyes, but he looked away quickly.

"You're okay then?" Chris asked. "How are you feeling?"

"I'm all right. Thanks to you," he said, bowing his head.

"He has a fractured rib," said Thomas. "Not my definition of all right."

"On a scale from good to dead, a fractured rib is much closer to all right than the other option," said Arnold, sitting up in his bedroll.

Chris noted that Arnold didn't seem to be struggling with his normal morning grogginess.

Nora, done with waking everyone, went to kneel by her pack. She pulled out her cooking equipment.

"So, what's your story?" asked Chris.

The boy—Brayden—bit his lip. "I was a crew member of a cargo ship, the *Silver Dragon*. We'd just left South Raec to return up the river to Coricstead when a storm drove us off course. We wrecked east of Rhetton. Some of the crew decided to returned north on foot, but bandits attacked us."

Terrin stopped her circling. "You're not what comes to mind when I think sailor."

Brayden glanced at her. "I'm stronger than I look."

"We're sorry for the deaths of your crewmates," said Chris. "I wish we'd arrived sooner. We're headed the opposite direction than you, but you're still welcome to stay with us, at least to the next town."

"No, I—" Brayden started, but paused. After considering for another moment he said, "I really need to go north. My family will be worried about me."

"That's quite a distance to go alone," said Thomas. "Injured, no less. You should at least stick around until your rib heals."

"Thomas is one of the best healers I've ever met," said Arnold. "He's even funny, at times."

"I really shouldn't," said Brayden, trying to stand. He paused, wincing, and sat back down. He glanced around the group, sighed, and said, "Very well."

Chris glanced over to Nora. "How long will breakfast take

to fix?"

"Maybe an hour," she mumbled.

Chris was surprised for a second. He'd forgotten how shy Nora was around people she'd just met. She'd bonded with Thomas quickly over their mutual interest in healing, but now that he thought about it, Chris hadn't noticed her interacting much with anyone else during their travels.

"All right, then. Thomas, would you ride down to the next village and buy a shovel or two?" Chris asked.

Thomas nodded and stood to saddle his horse. No one wanted, or needed, to question what those were for.

☙

Chris stood up as Arnold dropped another bandit's body next to the shallow hole they'd cleared in the brushy heath. He wiped sweat from his brow and glanced over at Brayden. Though everyone had vetoed his offer to help bury the bodies, the boy had found the strength to come say his final farewells to his crewmates.

Thomas had bought two shovels, so Chris and Terrin had started digging the graves. Thomas, Nora, and Arnold were separating the bandits from the sailors.

Brayden had walked past most of the bodies and stood for several minutes next to one short, stout man.

Now he'd moved away from the main group to where the final body lay.

☙

Brayden

In the sunlight, Brayden could see just how injured Reynard

was. He was willing to bet that the man had caused most of the bandit casualties. In the end, the bandit leader had cut his throat wide open, and though Reynard must have died immediately, the wound was thick with blood.

Brayden kneeled beside the body. None of the others were near, but he spoke softly.

"It was you, wasn't it? You must have found him in one of the towns we stopped at. I knew you didn't trust me, but I didn't think you'd turn me over like that."

His chest felt hollow.

"I suppose I should be angry. You made a bad choice, betrayed your own prince… but I respect your desire to protect your crew. I blame myself. If I'd tried harder to earn your trust… or if I'd fought better…"

He inhaled and forced himself to relax.

"In short, I forgive you, Reynard. I hope you're at rest."

Then he stood and dusted off his pants.

He looked over to where the others were working. His stomach flipped as his eyes settled on Chris. Or as he'd known him first: Honorable Christopher Fredrico, son of Earl Fredrico. Brayden had met Christopher years ago, back in the days before his self-imposed exile from his father's audience chamber. He couldn't mistake the man's pale blue eyes and curling black hair, and his build echoed that of his brother Gillian.

No longer "Honorable," though. And stripped of the name Fredrico when he was banished under threat of death for stealing the Fredricburg Shard.

At the time, there had been little proof of Chris's guilt.

Now a second Shard had gone missing, and why else would he still be in the country?

But why would he steal the Shards? They might have powerful

magic, but it was raw and dangerous—any magician who tried to use them would be sucked dry.

Unless Chris knew the real reason they were kept under guard.

"What have I gotten myself into?" he muttered.

❧ 20 ❧

Arnold

Arnold was floating again. This time he found himself in a wide, stone hallway. Tapestries and a couple doors lined one wall. Along the other, several evenly spaced openings let sunshine stream in. Old bowman's hollows, now glazed to form windows.

He glided forward to look through the closest one, and beneath him he could see a city, though he couldn't be sure what city from here—especially since it was blurred the same way irrelevant things had been in his previous dream.

Turning away, he started down the hall. He didn't know how long he wandered through the castle halls. Occasionally he passed nobles and ladies and a few servants. He could tell what they were by their clothes, but little more than that. He chose his path at random, taking stairs down toward the main floor whenever he found them.

Finally he heard voices muffled only by distance, not by the weird dream-fog. He approached slowly, rounding a couple bends.

"You've grown up so much. I wish you'd notice it," said a

woman's voice.

"You're just saying that." This second voice was of a young man. "I'm still clumsy, and politics goes over my head."

"You might not have noticed, but when the king summoned you to the court, you did just fine. And from the reports the ambassador sent us, it sounds like you helped out."

"Really? I'm pretty sure he hated me by the end of day two. He was practically jumping with glee when Father sent the letter to recall me."

"The report may have had some bias in its tone, but he's a professional. He related the events accurately."

Arnold rounded the last corner and saw the two strolling down the hall towards him, deep in their conversation. The woman wore a beautiful blue gown, laced with silver. Her braided hair coiled atop her head, encircled by a silver diadem studded with sapphires.

Beside her walked Brayden. He was no longer dressed in stained, torn clothes, but in well-pressed pants and shirt, with a black vest that looked like it might be silk. His brown hair was neatly combed.

"Mother, I think you're just as biased, if in the other way," said Brayden.

She laughed. It was one of those crystal bell laughs that, despite Arnold's shock at seeing Brayden here, made everything seem right. Once the woman stopped laughing, there was silence as they continued down the hall. As they passed Arnold, he turned to follow them.

He wasn't sure what to make of the scene. Between the crown and his vague memories of his one visit to Coricstead, he thought this must be the queen. But from what she'd said…

It occurred to him that the second prince was named Brayden.

But that meant they'd just saved the life of a prince. The

younger brother of the man who, under the king's authority, had banished Chris.

A prince who—for some reason—was pretending to be a simple sailor.

Why would he disguise himself? Had he recognized them? Arnold knew Chris had visited the king's court once with his family. If he recalled right, Brayden would have been no older than six or seven. It was doubtful they'd even met, or that the prince would have remembered.

Arnold winced. There was too much to take into consideration. It was too overwhelming. He shook his head to clear it. As he did so, the world blurred and vanished.

Arnold shot up, blinking away the last of the dream. The sun had already risen, and golden light dappled the tor. The smell of cooked oats wafted past his nose.

"Morning, sleepyhead," said Terrin. "Something wrong?"

Arnold glanced around their camp. The others were all awake, and his sudden movement had drawn their attention. He took one look at Brayden and made a decision.

"Everything is wrong," he said. "I had a nightmare about missing breakfast."

Terrin rolled her eyes, but the others laughed.

"It was a hammock's fault, no less," he added.

Terrin grimaced and spun away.

Nora handed him a bowl of porridge drizzled with honey. Everyone turned back to their meal, and Arnold relaxed.

It had been almost a week since Brayden had joined them. His ribs were healing quickly, and Arnold doubted Thomas could keep him here much longer, fractured rib or no.

Thinking back, Arnold realized the boy's recognizing they were fugitives would explain his original reluctance to stay with them. Though he had warmed up since then.

Even if he didn't know who they were now, he would soon. Thomas had warned them that the city was filled with wanted posters. The second Brayden returned home, he would see their faces.

He would tell the king, who would send a full troop after them.

Chris would be trapped.

But what could Arnold do about it?

He didn't even know whether to trust these foggy dreams. The first one had been wrong about the posters. Maybe this one was wrong about the boy.

"Arnold, want to duel?" Nora's soft words cut through his thoughts as gently as a knife through butter.

Arnold blinked in surprise. He noticed the empty bowl in his lap and realized his thoughts had carried him straight through breakfast. Since they'd stayed in the same camp for the last few days, things had become monotonous enough that it was easy to automatically fulfill simple tasks.

Arnold nodded. "Sure, let me get my hand first."

❧

"Break?" Arnold asked.

Nora nodded in agreement, swiping at her brow. "I can't believe it's almost noon. Before, I could only duel a few minutes at a time."

"You've improved. I think you have some of that Yorc talent helping you out," Arnold said. The mountain men of Yorc were notorious warriors.

Nora laughed.

As she went to prepare lunch, Arnold took one look around

the campsite, and decided this was as alone as he and Brayden would get. Thomas had gone to restock herbs, Terrin was off hunting, and Chris had left to refill their water skins. He didn't know what he planned on saying, but this way there'd be fewer people to see his embarrassment if he made a fool of himself.

He walked over and sat next to the boy, keeping his face pointed straight ahead and tilted up, only watching Brayden's reaction from the corner of his eyes.

"Do you trust us?" Arnold asked.

"I… guess?" Brayden's brow furrowed. "I mean, you saved my life, and… well, you've all done more for me than most people would for a stranger. You have given me no reason *not* to trust you. Why do you ask?"

"Because…"

Arnold paused. It didn't seem right to just blurt out that he knew who Brayden was, and how could he explain that his brother, Prince Tyler, had gotten everything wrong?

"I…"

Brayden raised an eyebrow. "Is this the start of one of your bad jokes? You're going to confess to being a dragon in disguise, or something?"

Arnold's mouth dropped open as he feigned offense. "Brayden! How could you not love my jokes? They're the best."

Brayden grinned. "That's one way to put it."

Arnold chuckled, but shook his head. "No, that's not it at all. I… I wanted to make sure you knew that we are good people. Chris, especially. And loyal to our country… and to our king."

Good job, Arnold. That doesn't sound creepy at all.

Brayden's grin vanished. He drew his knees closer to his chest so he could drape his arms across them. They sat there for a minute, the boy gazing off into the distance, Arnold trying to look anywhere but at him.

"If I didn't know better," Brayden said, "I'd think you were accusing me of being a fugitive… and threatening to turn me in."

He does know, Arnold realized.

"No," he said. "Even if we thought you were a fugitive, having known you… well, I, at least, could never imagine you committing any crime. We are loyal, but we understand that even the king might make a mistake."

"I'm not sure you should say that in front of him."

"Probably not."

"Lunch is ready," called Nora.

Arnold jumped to his feet. "Thank goodness. I'm starved."

❧ 21 ❧

Trillory

"Magic lessons are great and all, but not much beats a nice ride," Trill said as she slipped her feet from the stirrups and slid to the ground.

"Does that make magic lessons while riding the perfect activity? If so, I suppose I'm the master planner of days," said Eric, dismounting his own horse.

"I suppose so." Trill bobbed a quick curtsy. "It's an honor to make your acquaintance, Sir Day-Planner."

"Ooh, I like that. You should call me that from now on."

"Uh, no." Trill turned away to start untacking her horse.

When they finished, they took a stroll through the garden before entering the manor.

"Walk with me to the audience chamber?" Eric offered his arm.

"Why not?" Trill said. "As long as you don't expect me to stick around."

She took his arm, but they'd only rounded one corner when she pulled away, shocked to see her brother Anthony standing at the end of the hall.

He and Chris shared curly black hair and blue eyes, but they were different in every other way. Anthony, the eldest, was power hungry and a bully, spoiled by their father and the duke. He had especially enjoyed harassing Chris, and she could never forgive that.

Anthony glanced up at them and smiled. After bowing, he approached. "Sir Eric, Trillory. I'm glad to see you're both in good health."

Trill's back had gone rigid. "Anthony. You've returned. I trust your journey went well?"

"Yes, yes. Everything is in order," said Anthony.

"I suppose you won't divulge where you went?" asked Trill, lifting her chin to meet his eyes.

Anthony's snaky-fake smile spread across his face. "I see no reason to. What is it to you?"

"Well, you are my beloved brother," said Trill. Her icy voice seemed sharp, even in her throat. "Why shouldn't I take an interest in your activities? Especially when you leave me here alone, suddenly and without explanation."

"It seems to me that you're hardly alone. In fact, you look like you're in excellent hands." He nodded at Eric.

Trill glanced at Eric, who was smiling weakly. His eyes shifted back and forth between her and Anthony.

She tossed her head. "That might be, but it doesn't change that I might have been worried about my brother. You didn't even say when you'd be back."

"Because I didn't know. But I'm back now. Are you happy?"

"No." *I would rather you'd stayed gone.*

"Well, then, while your attempts to annoy me are amusing, I have more important things to be attending to." Anthony faced

Eric. "Sir Eric, it seems you've done an excellent job in your father's absence, though I'm sure you'll be glad to know that he'll return soon."

With that, Anthony spun and disappeared down the hall.

Trill growled, her hands tightening into fists.

"Are you okay Trill?" Eric touched her wrist lightly.

She shut her eyes, forcing herself to take several deep breaths and relax. "Yes. It's just that Anthony always annoys me to no end. I'd almost forgotten that he lived here, too."

"Anthony isn't that bad," said Eric. "Though I haven't seen him like that before."

"He is adept at hiding it," said Trill. Then she shook her head. "Well, I certainly don't intend to let him ruin my mood."

"I wonder how he knows Father will be back soon," Eric mused. "It raises a slight problem."

"Oh?"

Eric lowered his voice as he continued. "Unless you want him to find out about your having magic, you shouldn't come to the practice room for a while. He sometimes stops by to see how I'm doing."

Trill lowered her eyes. "That is a problem." Then she brightened and said, "Well, I guess that means more riding lessons, O Sir Day-Planner."

Eric laughed. "I suppose it does."

☙

Christopher

After spending two weeks on a hill, Chris didn't mind losing a couple more days to escort Brayden north, but every step back towards Coricstead made him uneasy. Thomas had insisted, though, on seeing his patient travel before they abandoned him.

In different circumstances, Chris would have gladly taken the boy all the way to his doorstep. But it was time to part ways. Farewells circled around the party as Brayden thanked them all for helping him out.

"Thomas, Nora, thank you for all your work healing me, and your delicious meals."

Nora smiled, a soft rose color touching her cheeks.

"It was a pleasure," said Thomas. "Just take care of those ribs. Remember to breathe deeply. And don't blame me if they get worse because you've pushed yourself too hard."

Brayden nodded before turning away.

"Terrin," he continued, "thank you for shooting that monster before he skewered me."

"I have no problem with killing monsters," said Terrin.

Brayden raised his eyebrow and moved on.

"Arnold, thank you for… keeping things interesting."

"What, that's all I get?" Arnold pouted. "How about, 'Thank you for your awesomely inspirational swordsmanship when you rushed to my aid'?"

Brayden frowned. "I… guess."

Arnold laughed and patted the boy's shoulder. "Just kidding. Safe journey."

As Arnold stepped back, Brayden turned to Chris.

"And thank you, Chris, for everything. I… I wish you all the luck possible in your travels."

"I wish we could have done more," said Chris, shaking Brayden's hand. "Be safe on your way to the capital."

Brayden stepped back away, and the five of them mounted their horses. They started down the hill, backs turned to Brayden. It occurred to Chris that it was unlikely they'd meet the boy again.

Just like all the other people they'd met in their travels and come to think of as friends.

He turned back to wave at Brayden one last time.

Then his chest constricted as he realized what the scene must look like from the boy's perspective. Five people on horseback, riding downhill towards the rising sun.

It was the last dream he'd had. At the time, he'd thought he'd parted ways with Arnold, Terrin, and Nora for good, so the vision had made little sense, and he'd forgotten about it. But now it came back, clear as ever.

So they were still on the right track, following the magic's cryptic trail. That was good to know.

But what about the one other dream that had yet to come true? Though it had been foggy, and he couldn't remember any of his surroundings, the feeling of danger and his need to stop those mysterious people at any cost had been just as vivid as the other vision-dreams.

The memories of when he'd awakened to discover he'd nearly choked Nora were also vivid. He didn't know, or understand, what had happened in that dream. But he knew that the last thing he wanted was for it to come true.

❦ 22 ❦

Terrin

The first thing they saw on Dawncliff was the lighthouse, visible on the horizon while they were still miles away. Even from that distance, Terrin could tell it was old, though not quite ancient.

When the plains people had come across the ocean from the west, they'd spread through the land quickly, reaching the eastward side of North Raec within three generations. The earliest settlements made a focus on fishing, so lighthouses had been built, here and other places.

She smiled. Most forest people wouldn't know things like that. They cared little for history. Frankly, so did she, but the plainsmen thought it was important, and she'd had to memorize it and many other useless facts.

This lighthouse, though, was a more recent addition, its predecessor having been destroyed a few hundred years ago. Her history professor hadn't mentioned how.

As they came closer to the cliff, Terrin saw the stone formations

Arnold had told them about. They were unnatural-looking pillars, scattered across the cliff. They rose from the ground like trees—twisting bulbous things. But there was a pattern to their shapes, with similar proportions between widths and heights, and the odd protrusions coming from similar places.

As they reached the first one, a mile from the lighthouse and the actual cliff, she could see how it might be thought similar to a soldier standing watch. With an oddly shaped head and ripples on top that could be hair. And that bit could be a sword resting on his shoulders, with ridges hinting at clothes.

Though the sun was high and bright overhead, the cliff top had a somber feel to it. The grass looked more gray than green, and sparser than before. The standing stones sent strange shadows across the gaps between them.

She noticed more details on the statues as they went further—expressions, stances, even a dagger in one's boot—till they appeared more and more like warriors frozen in time. As they drew near the lighthouse, the gentle roar of waves against the rocks below the cliff grew.

"Wait," said Chris from the front. The group stopped and waited as he turned Marc back to face them. "Where exactly are we going?"

There was a long silence.

Terrin shrugged. "How should we know? None of us have been here before."

"Well, having seen the place, I agree with Arnold that the next riddle must be here," said Chris. "But where do we start? There's nowhere for it to be hidden."

Terrin looked around. She'd been so interested in the soldiers that she'd almost forgotten their purpose in being here. But with the riddle in mind, nothing stood out. No caves, no walls to hold secret doors, no super trees, and none of the statues seemed special.

"We could ask the locals. There has to be someone who lights the lighthouse," said Nora. Her voice sounded quieter than ever in this haunted place, or perhaps the waves drowned it out. "We've needed the help of others before."

"I'd agree, except we're trying to avoid people," said Chris. "We'll keep that as a last resort."

"What about magic?" volunteered Arnold. "The other riddles all reeked of magic, and Terrin's got her magic senses. If we wander enough, maybe she can feel something."

"I'm willing to try," she said. "But even if I sense it, that doesn't mean we're near the entrance. The second riddle was pretty far from the entrance to its cave."

"It's our best bet," said Chris. "Though it's going to be interesting, searching all these statues."

"We should spread out," said Thomas. "There's a chance the way is marked by the statues somehow, but there must be a couple hundred."

"Alright," said Chris. "Terrin, you head further towards the cliff. Nora and Arnold, you two go right, and Thomas and I will go left from here."

She nodded and had just turned Leaf toward her assigned search area when a voice called, "Hello. Can I help you?"

Terrin stiffened, Chris's shoulders twitched, and Nora jumped, making Minty toss her head and snort.

They turned to see a young woman standing on a balcony-like porch that wrapped around the outside of the lighthouse, overlooking the statues. She wore a light blue summer dress that flapped gently in the breeze. She waved at them, and even from this distance Terrin could see the girl's smile.

"So much for avoiding people," said Terrin.

"Maybe she's waving to the other mysterious and out of place group of adventurers?" offered Arnold.

Terrin glared at him.

"What do we do now?" Thomas asked, looking at Chris.

Chris took a deep breath. Then he said, "It is what it is. It would look strange if we ignore her."

He waved to the girl and signaled Marc to walk towards her.

After a couple minutes of weaving through the statues, which got thicker the closer they came to the lighthouse, they arrived beneath the porch.

The girl was still waiting, leaning against the railing with her arms crossed on top of it. Her blue eyes sparkled, and her dark blond hair looked like it was dancing in the wind, rather than being twisted and tangled. She was perhaps in her early twenties, but she had an air of childish joy about her.

"Hello," said Chris.

"Welcome. What brings you out this way? We don't get many visitors out here."

"We had heard about the stones here looking like warriors and wanted to see for ourselves."

"Yes, they are a bit famous. Mother knows a lot of stories about them, if you want to come in. We have lemonade."

"We're stopping," said Arnold, before Chris could say anything. "Definitely stopping."

Terrin sighed.

"All right. I know better than to stand between you and lemonade," said Chris, laughing.

"There's a place to tie your horses around the side, over there." The woman pointed.

Terrin dismounted and tied Leaf next to Rich. As she and Arnold headed for the steps, she nudged him with her elbow and whispered, "Child."

He stuck his tongue out at her, then grinned.

Inside the lighthouse, spiral stairs led both up to the beacon room and down to the basement. At the center of the spacious room stood a round table and its four chairs. The sun filtered through arched windows that studded the back wall, and over time it had bleached the wood floor. To the left a door led to a second room.

A counter ran around the back wall, with a small stove built into the stone. Over the stove, an older version of the girl stirred a pot. Her hair had started to gray, but, as she looked up at the newcomers, the same smile lit her face.

"Hello, there. It's so nice to see some unfamiliar faces."

The younger woman disappeared into the other room, then reappeared with an extra chair. "Make yourselves comfortable, I'll get the lemonade, as promised." This time she pranced down the stairs to the basement.

The woman stepped away from the pot and retrieved five glasses from the cupboards beneath the counter. As she set them out around the table, the group took their seats.

"I'm afraid we can't offer much more than lemonade. There's just the two of us here, and we don't get visitors often enough to prepare extra food."

"It's fine," said Chris. "We weren't expecting even this much hospitality."

"You're too kind. It's the least we can do." The woman beamed at him. "I'm Meredith, by the way. And my daughter is Leah."

The girl returned, clutching a giant stone pitcher that dripped with condensation. Arnold jumped to his feet to take it from her. Even with one hand, he lifted it from her arms easily.

"Thank you," she said, her cheeks reddening. "Though I'm

sorry to make a guest work."

"On the contrary. I can't let a woman do the heavy lifting."

"That does raise a question," Thomas said. "Isn't it dangerous for two women like yourselves to live out here alone?"

Meredith's smile faltered. "Well, not so much. The lighthouse is out of the way of most people, and, if you're not expecting them, the statues can be quite scary."

Terrin nodded. Even knowing about them, she'd found the stones unsettling.

The woman continued, "If we do encounter trouble, though, there's a nice little town not far north from here. Leah's uncle lives there, he stops by every so often. Everyone else there thinks this place is cursed, though." She laughed.

"Cursed?" asked Terrin, leaning forward.

"There's an idea that once you've stayed here, you can never leave. The previous caretakers for the lighthouse went to visit family in Coricstead, and they all died from the plague during its first sweep. And then when it struck again…"

Meredith's voice faltered, and Leah stepped forward to finish. "My father and brother had gone to a market week in a large town west of here and died of the second plague."

"I'm so sorry," said Terrin, covering her mouth.

Arnold froze, the pitcher hovering above Nora's glass.

Thomas had bowed his head.

"I lost my wife and much of my family to the two plagues," he said. "It is a hard way to see your loved ones go. It must be even harder not getting to say farewell or offer comfort on their way out."

He lifted his head and gave Meredith and Leah a watery smile. Glistening tears welled in their eyes.

Arnold

Arnold sipped his lemonade, listening as Meredith and Thomas shared memories of their respective spouses, with Leah occasionally inserting a comment. Though Thomas was always ready to share his medical insight in the form of a story or joke, Arnold hadn't realized how little the man talked about himself.

"After the Healer's Guild threw me out, I returned to Charlon." Thomas wrapped up his story. "I was hoping to meet up with some old friends, but they had moved on. I inherited a decent sum of money. So I used it to follow my other love, exploring the history behind legends. I joined up with these young folks, and now I find myself in this amazing place."

"John loved it here," said Meredith. She sighed. "We'd come down every few weeks. He liked to wander among the statues and give them names and stories. He told me they were soldiers that fled here during the first Raecan War. They tried to protect the lighthouse—the original building—but a powerful mage cursed them to stone. Sometimes he'd even say that the mage tore down the tower and trapped them in the very thing they were trying to protect."

Arnold glanced around, trying to imagine the stones being torn apart and wrapped around the soldiers.

Could a mage really do something like that?

"I never believed it was possible," Meredith continued. "But when he talked about it, his eyes would just light up. He was ecstatic when we were offered the care of the lighthouse."

Laughter bubbled from her chest as she added, "He would even talk to the eagle."

Chris's head snapped up, and he blurted out, "Eagle?"

It took Arnold a second to make the connection that Chris had. The last riddle had mention a "great one" soaring high above the water, which they'd assumed to mean there were eagles living around the cliff.

"Oh, yes," said Meredith. "There's an eagle that's been here as long as anyone remembers. She has a nest in a cleft partway down the cliff-face. Sometimes she'll even land on the lighthouse balcony and say hello. Not so much since John died, but she's been warming up to Leah."

"Isn't it dangerous, being that close to an eagle?" asked Terrin.

Arnold agreed. He liked animals as much as the next person, but this sounded as stupid as trying to tame a full-grown wolf.

"Uncle always says that, too," said Leah. "But she's never attacked anyone. And like Mother said, Father could spend hours talking with her. If you stick around long, I'm sure you'll see her. She's off hunting now, but she usually comes back after lunch."

Chris rubbed the dark beard he'd been unable to shave since he left River's Cross. At first it hadn't been too bad, but now it looked ridiculous. Arnold was glad his own beard was taking a slower approach to its growth.

"Could we see the eagle's nest?" Chris asked.

"I suppose," said Meredith. "You have to be careful not to fall, and there's not much to see. But Leah can show you."

"I think I'll sit this one out," said Thomas.

Chris nodded, and the remaining four friends stood. Leah hopped to her feet and led the way out of the lighthouse, down the creaking wooden steps, through the warrior statues, and to the edge of the cliff.

"It's just below there." Leah pointed. "I recommend lying down and approaching the cliff on your stomach. It's uncomfortable, but it's better than falling."

"Terrin?" Chris said, glancing at her.

Terrin nodded. She walked within a few feet of the cliff before crouching then lying down to peer over the edge. She pulled back and shook her head violently.

"What?" asked Arnold, stepping towards her.

"Nothing. Just reminded me of a bad memory." Terrin stood and brushed off her pants.

"Well?" asked Chris.

Terrin nodded at him. "There's definitely magic down there."

"Magic?" said Leah, her crystal-like eyes growing large. "You mean, the cliffs *are* cursed?"

"Don't worry," said Chris. "It's harmless, I'm sure."

"Was it left behind by the mage that cursed all the statues?"

"No," said Chris. "Well… I don't think so." He paused, his eyes glazing as he sunk deep into thought.

Arnold rolled his eyes. "This is silly. We might as well explain. We're following the riddles that King Miles followed in his hunt for the Riddled Stone, and we think one's here."

"I'm almost positive." Terrin nodded. "The magic felt the same as the other riddles."

"Oh," said Leah. "That's... interesting." Then she brightened and laughed. "Father would have been thrilled to learn that the cliffs have historical fame."

Arnold raised an eyebrow. "Most people would be curious," he said, "or doubtful, or something."

Leah shrugged. "I just don't see that it's that important. Miles's journey was impressive, but it was hundreds of years ago. What does it matter where he found the Stone, or whether he followed magical riddles? And it's not like we need to re-find the Stone. It's safe in the king's palace, right?"

"That is rather practical," said Terrin. "One has to wonder if there will be any sort of big discovery at the end of this quest. Or whether it'll have been a lot of walking to and fro for nothing."

"I guess we'll see when we get there," said Chris. Then he narrowed his eyes at her. "I thought you were over that?"

"I am. I just think Leah raises a valid point."

"So, if the riddle's down there, how are we going to reach it?" asked Arnold.

"We could rappel," said Nora. "Do we have enough rope?"

"Probably," said Chris. He glanced around. "How many feet would we need if we tied it to that statue?" He gestured to one of the stones and glanced at Terrin.

She tilted her head. "Maybe a hundred to hundred-fifty. The cleft is about thirty feet down the cliff."

"All right. Terrin and I will go get the rope."

"And gloves," Nora called after them as they jogged back to the lighthouse where they'd left their bags.

"Are you really going down there?" said Leah. "It's dangerous. The eagle will be back soon, and she will not take kindly to her nest being invaded. She's friendly, but defensive. I've seen her chase off other birds before."

"We'll just have to hurry." Arnold smiled at her.

After a few minutes, Chris and Terrin returned, carrying several cords of ropes, tied together. Terrin took one end and knotted it around the stone warrior closest to the cliff's edge.

"Chris obviously has to go," said Nora. "But is it safe for him to go alone?"

"I don't see why not," said Chris. "You guys will be up here to watch the rope, so it's not like I need someone to catch me. And we don't know how much room there will be down there. With any luck, it'll be a quick trip down and back up."

Arnold grimaced. He wanted more than anything to go, too. At the last riddle, the tree itself had attacked them. He hated to think what kind of protection this riddle had.

"But if you get hurt somehow?" said Nora. "Or if it is a deeper cave?"

"If it is, then Terrin can come down after me," said Chris.

"All right, but it should be me, not Terrin," said Nora. "I have experience with climbing cliffs."

Arnold grinned. Like Chris, he thought Terrin the better partner in case of a fight. But the rare sight of Nora being stubborn amused him.

Chris hesitated, then shook his head and sighed. "Fine. If there's an actual cave, then you can come down after me. For now, let's make a harness for this thing." He held up the rope.

ↀ

Christopher

A few minutes later, Chris hung on the side of the cliff, gripping the rope so tight his knuckles hurt. Though it didn't look that far from up above, now it felt like hundreds of feet as he took careful backwards steps down the rocks. The harness they'd made was rather uncomfortable, which didn't help the climb to seem any faster.

Finally, his feet touched solid ground. Though he'd forced himself to continue breathing through the entire descent, his whole body had become rigid, and the pressure beneath his heels was like a trigger for his muscles to relax.

He looked around the platform. Nine feet across, the eagle's nest left him little room to stand.

The cleft did carve deeper into the cliff, opening into a shadowy corridor. The magic swelled towards him, then moved back. It felt like the cave was breathing. He glanced at the sea to confirm his suspicion that the motion kept time with the waves of water.

With a sigh, he removed the harness and called up for Nora to come down and join him.

It took them a minute to prepare a second harness for her, but he noted that she was right about her skill at climbing cliffs. She moved down it with little hesitation and seemed unphased when she dropped the last couple feet to the edge.

Chris took the torch she'd brought and lit it before the two ventured further into the cave.

The passage wound through the cliff, about a hundred yards long, its wall and floor perfectly smooth. It was too narrow to walk comfortably side by side, so Chris led the way. He rounded the last corner and almost stumbled into the riddle. He stepped back and let Nora come up beside him.

At the center of a small room sat a smooth hump of rock, as if it had risen from the ground. Etched in its surface were strange symbols, just like the other riddles—words only Chris could read. He took a deep breath, then whispered.

"South of where thy enemies dwell,
Where traitors plot of evil deeds,
You'll find the fifth guardian.
Fear his paws, his claws are sharp.
He roams where man is feared to go.
In the open you'll find that he defends
Where next your journey takes you."

Chris stared at the riddle a few minutes longer. Like the previous clues, it had burned itself into his mind, tempting him to stop right there and consider what it meant.

Nora tugged his hand. "The others are waiting."

He nodded and turned to follow her out of the cave.

As they exited the cave, he noticed that Nora gave a sigh of relief and swiftly put the harness back on. Ropes secured, she caught hold of the cliff wall to start her climb back up.

Chris waited till she had topped the cliff before pulling his own harness into place and reaching for the first handhold.

"The eagle!" Leah's high-pitched shout pierced through his eardrums—and his stomach.

PART THREE

❦ 24 ❦

Arnold, 10 Years Earlier

Arnold's feet scuffed against the bricks of the road. In the distance, thunder rumbled, and the menacing clouds above had chased most people off the streets. In one hand, he gripped a small bag of slowly cooling roasted chestnuts. To his right rose a fence, through which he could see the city garden. Several times he glanced over at the hedges and flower beds, but he continued to circle it, passing three entrances before he sighed and turned in.

Without looking where he was going, he wandered a circuitous route through the park, only stopping when a squirrel dashed across his path.

He tilted his head to watch it run under a hedge. It clutched a small nut in its mouth and clawed furiously at the soft dirt.

He watched it for a minute, then he crouched and pulled a chestnut from the bag he'd been ignoring. "Hey buddy," he breathed, and leaned out to place the nut a foot from the squirrel.

The squirrel snapped alert, looking first at him and then the nut.

Arnold braced his arms against his knees and remained still as he stared to the side of the squirrel.

"I hope your day's been good." Arnold said. "This weather isn't great, is it? Chris's sick, so I have no one to cause trouble with. There's already a test in our first week back at school. Not to mention Terrin—of all people, Terrin—found out I can't stand spiders."

The squirrel crept forward to snatch up the nut. Arnold continued talking as he pulled out another nut and extended it, balanced at the tip of his fingers.

"So far she's mocked me every time I've seen her, but it's only a matter of time until she plants one in my room. I bet she loves spiders. There's probably hundreds in Xell Forest.

"Do you know how annoying it is to listen to how things work in Xell? Like I care how they live way over on the other side of the country. She—well, Chris—says she came to learn about our culture, so she could become a go-between for our two people. But she spends all her time talking about how great her people are compared to us.

"I mean, I thought we were all North Raecans, under the same king. Why do we even need a go-between?"

The squirrel had taken the second chestnut and was now staring at him with its twinkling black eyes. Arnold gradually pulled back his hand to grab the chestnut bag and place it near the squirrel, then finally let his eyes fall on the squirrel directly as it filled its paws and mouth with as many nuts as it could carry.

"School was okay before Terrin showed up, and I thought this year I'd just ignore her, but the mere sight of her makes me mad," said Arnold. "So now this whole place stinks. I thought Father understood that, but he continues to insist I come here. Mother dies, and suddenly she's right about everything."

Arnold's fists clenched. The squirrel gave him a quick, wide-eyed look before it fled under the hedge and out of sight.

"Thanks for letting me rant," Arnold said, picking up his bag to continue on his way.

He did feel better. His feet still scuffed against the path, but he lifted his chin, and his eyes flitted back and forth, observing the plant life.

A bird chirped, and he turned to see an early junco atop a hedge, inches from where the shrubbery broke to allow the path deeper into the park. He watched the bird. Mother had loved juncos, the males specifically, with their smooth, black feathers and white bellies. Even during winter, she'd sit in the garden for hours, just watching them and the other birds.

Arnold sighed and had turned away when he heard soft crying from through the hedge. He froze.

Unable to fight his curiosity, he turned and crept to the corner of the hedge, peering around. There was a clearing, decorated by a small pond. Across the pond, curled in a tight ball on a bench, sat Terrin, her back trembling with her sobs.

Arnold froze, mouth agape. His mind had gone blank, and he wasn't sure how long he stood there, just staring, until he dragged himself to his senses and backed away.

The junco burst from the hedge with a flurry of feathers, and he glanced at it. When he looked back, he was looking straight into Terrin's rich, brown eyes.

Her eyes glistened, partly from tears, but also with rage. He thought he could hear her teeth grinding together.

She stood, tossing her disheveled hair over her shoulder, and her jaw jutted out towards him like a sword. "Go ahead. Mock me. Call me a crybaby, you childish lout. I'm sure you've got all sorts of jabs based on your own uninformed assumptions."

She blinked, and one last tear ran over her sharp cheek bone and to her chin where it trembled.

Arnold snapped his mouth shut, only for it to fall open again. His mind was reeling, wondering why Terrin, of all people Terrin, would be crying. Wasn't she the stubborn forest girl who loved school to death?

Unless she didn't. He didn't know her all that well. Just that every time they met, they ended up fighting, and that her main resource for insults was her superior intelligence.

The two glared at each other for another few minutes. The tear dropped free and plopped to the ground. Swallowing hard, Terrin raised her arm to rub her face.

"I'm sorry," Arnold yelped. Then he spun and dashed down the path.

He stopped after going only a few feet. He stood, forcing himself to take deep breaths for a minute. Then he tiptoed back to the clearing.

Terrin had crumpled at the edge of the pond, staring at it. Two tears dropped to the water. She rubbed her eyes, then shook her head. It had the opposite effect from what she wanted, and more tears welled in the corners of her eye.

Arnold pulled away, wondering what to do. His experience with crying was minimal. After his mother's death, he had heard his father crying in his room, but the servants had insisted that acknowledging it would only end in disaster, and his father had recovered quickly and shown no sign of crying again. Judging from that evidence, it would be better to leave and pretend this never happened.

A hollow feeling clawed at his chest. Terrin's stubborn nature reminded him of his father's. But he also remembered how, following the death of his mother, he'd spent many nights sobbing into his pillow so no one would notice, but all the same wishing there *was* someone there to notice and comfort him.

He'd tried, with some success, distracting himself with training, but that was a temporary fix. He'd longed for Mother's warm embrace, her musical voice easing him with stories about the habits of field mice and voles. There was no one who could replace her.

No one he trusted to replace her. Anyone else would have just laughed at him.

The way Terrin expected him to laugh at her.

Arnold braced himself for whatever reaction Terrin gave him and leaped into the clearing with a cartwheel.

Terrin looked up blankly as he entered hands first. With a deep breath, he bent his arm so he collapsed to the ground. Without even blinking, he rolled into the water.

Terrin scrambled back as he plunged into the pond, sending water splashing everywhere.

He gasped as he realized just how cold and murky the water was, immediately regretting his decision. He thrashed, searching for the water's surface. Slimy fish brushed against him as they attempted to escape. With all the mud stirred up, the surface was even harder to find.

Two wiry arms plunged into the water, grabbed his arm, and with surprising strength dragged him to the surface. His head broke through, and he choked for breath. Terrin kept pulling him towards the edge, though now he was reoriented, his feet easily touched the bottom of the pond.

He exited the water only partway before collapsing on the

grass, liquid streaming from his hair and clothes.

"What did you think you were doing, you nitwit?" asked Terrin. As soon as he had reached safety, she'd stood to plant her hands on her hips.

"Well," said Arnold. "It seemed like a good plan at the time. If I'd spent more than half a second thinking about it, I might have realized just how cold the water would be. But for a half-second plan, it did pretty well."

"Plan? What plan? To embarrass yourself completely?"

Arnold considered this, then shrugged. "I mean, it worked. You stopped crying."

"Huh?" Terrin stared at him.

Arnold sat up and squeezed the water from his shirt.

"It's not right for you to cry," he said. "You're supposed to be the intimidating Forest Girl, fearless and stubborn, with an emotional range from indifferent to angry. Crying made you look fragile."

Terrin crossed her arms. "So just because I don't let others see how I feel, that means I feel nothing?"

Arnold met her eyes. He blinked, then puckered his lips in a fish face.

Terrin frowned. "What are you doing?"

"I've decided to make a fish face whenever I realize I agree with you on something. Like, how we shouldn't judge each other, based on our surface actions, to be feelingless jerks. Though, I don't really understand why you were crying."

"Like you would," snapped Terrin. "You're here among your own people. Everyone likes you, and no one constantly harasses you because he's too childish to realize how hurtful his insults are."

Arnold hung his head. "I'm sorry. I was absorbed by how much I didn't want to be here to realize that you're even more out of place."

"Like your apology now means anything." Terrin tossed her hair and turned away. "I'm going back to school."

"Do you really not have friends?" asked Arnold as she started away.

She stopped, turning only partway back. "It's none of your business."

Arnold made a fish face again.

Terrin rolled her eyes. "I knew you were childish. I didn't realize you were an idiot. You should go back, too, before you catch cold in those clothes."

"Can't we talk? I want to help you. I don't want you to cry anymore."

Terrin faced him and squared her shoulders. "Why would you care? You're the main reason I hate it here. You do nothing but harass me, and anyone who might have gotten over me being an outsider doesn't want to get on yours or Chris's bad side."

"Because… no one helped me," said Arnold. "My mother was killed by bandits two summers ago. I love my father, and the servants and the other knights and squires are amazing, but they only see me as my father's son. None of them are people I could open up to."

"So you thought, to cheer me up, you'd drown yourself? You annoy me, but not so much that seeing you die would bring me pleasure."

"Well… Mother always said laughter was the best medicine. And I figured, if I opened my mouth, we'd end up in a fight instead."

"Laughter? It wasn't funny, it was stupid."

"I didn't know you cared so much." Arnold jumped forward to hug her. She shrieked, trying to escape. "I knew we were secretly friends all along."

"Let go. You're getting me wet. If you don't let go, I'll never talk to you again, you weirdo. Like I'd be friends with you."

Arnold released her.

"Chris is going to be so surprised when he gets over his cold, and we're best friends." He laughed.

"Stop saying things like that." Terrin elbowed him in the ribs, and he doubled over. "Honestly! If you've been that desperate for my friendship, you should have asked."

❧ 25 ❧

Nora

If it were not for Chris hanging mere feet from its nest, Nora would have found the eagle fascinating. It seemed bigger than the eagles she'd seen in the northern mountains. Its feathers gleamed, and its talons glinted in the sun.

"Climb, Chris," shouted Terrin. Nora noticed the forest girl's eyes flick to the lighthouse, where she'd left her bow.

The eagle wheeled over them once, then glided out away from the cliff. It turned back and screeched at Chris. Then it pitched forward, diving at him.

"No!" cried Leah, stepping towards the cliff. "Friend, please." She stretched out her hand towards the bird. The eagle banked for a second, looking at the girl.

Terrin's gaze snapped to Leah. "What are you doing?"

"It's coming this way. Get back from the edge," yelled Arnold.

The eagle shot towards them like an arrow, aiming straight at Leah. The girl's back trembled, but she didn't move.

Nora stepped out to grab Leah's shoulder and pull her back

145

from the edge.

"Don't touch her!" said Terrin.

"Wha—" Nora started, but Arnold leaped in front of them all, drawing his sword and pointing the blade towards the bird.

"No! Don't hurt her." Leah shouted, seizing Arnold's arm to force the sword back.

"Leah," said Arnold. He jumped sideways, dropping his sword to pull Leah with him, as the eagle shot straight through where he'd been standing.

Nora ducked, and she felt its talons brush her hair.

"Leah, the bird could have killed us," said Arnold.

"You mustn't hurt her," said Leah. Tears sprung to her eyes. "She's my father's friend. *My* friend."

The eagle circled above them again.

"Arnold," said Terrin. "Let Leah distract the bird."

"What?" his fist clenched. "She'll get hurt. I don't care how sentimental she is, that eagle's angry."

Terrin bit her lip. "I… trust me. Please."

Nora glanced at Leah, then at the bird circling above, wondering what Terrin was thinking.

"It's coming again," she said as the bird dove.

"Leah, talk to her," said Terrin.

Arnold scooted over to grab his sword, but Leah pulled herself to her feet and turned to look at the eagle.

"Please. We aren't your enemies. You know me, I'm your friend. Please, just this once, let us pass."

The bird slowed to swerve around Leah. The girl turned to follow it and put her arm out, her delicate hand palm up. "I am your friend. You know I would never let you be hurt. Trust me."

The eagle whistled, wheeling sharply over Leah, and then alighted on the girl's arm.

Nora's mouth dropped open, Arnold raised his sword, but Leah showed no pain. Instead, a smile filled her face.

"Thank you," she said to the bird.

"Wow." Chris's voice called Nora's attention to the cliff, where Chris was just pulling himself over the top.

She looked back in time to see Leah lift her arm, springing the eagle back into the air. The eagle screeched again, then dove below the cliff's edge.

"What was that?" asked Arnold, sheathing his sword.

"I don't know," said Leah, rubbing her arm. "It was like she didn't have weight, or talons."

"It was magic," said Terrin. "Leah's a magician."

"What?" Leah said with a bemused smile. "But... but magicians don't exist, not anymore."

"What you just did was magic," Terrin said. "Didn't you feel any sort of... tingling?"

"Yes," said Leah. "But that happens all the time."

"And what about in the eagle's nest? Do you feel it from there, too?"

"You mean, that feeling like the cleft is breathing? That's what magic feels like?"

Terrin nodded.

"But... how can I be a magician?"

"Magicians are very real," said Chris. "I've known a couple. They're just rare. Your magic probably saved my life," he added. "Thank you."

"I think I need to sit down," said Leah. She turned and drifted back towards the lighthouse.

"So, you just hoped her 'magic' would protect her from the eagle?" said Arnold, turning towards Terrin.

"She was using it subconsciously when she called to the eagle the first time. So I gave her space to do what came naturally to her."

"It was still dangerous. What would we have said to Meredith? 'Sorry, we stepped out for ten minutes and got your daughter critically wounded'?"

"I trusted her judgment," said Terrin. "And that you'd step in, if anything went wrong. You're good at that."

Nora met Chris's eyes and said, "We should go make sure Leah's okay. She must be confused. It's not every day you discover that you have magical abilities."

＠ 26 ＠

Brayden

Brayden's chest heaved with gasps for breath. He held his left hand against his mouth, trying to stifle the sound. He crouched, and his back pressed against something hard. His entire body trembling, he tried to brace his other hand against the ground, but there was something in it that he couldn't make his fingers release.

He looked down and saw he was clutching a knife. Hardened blood covered his entire hand. The knife dripped with red. His eyes traced the blade to the tip, which was buried in the face of the assassin.

He screamed, jumping away from the blood-covered body. He tried to throw the knife away from himself, but his fingers still wouldn't release it.

"Funny, isn't it?" said a voice behind him. He spun to see Reynard standing there. A sword dangled from his hand, its tip scraping the ground. A hole gaped in the man's neck, but he talked with just the slightest rasp. "You killed a trained assassin without blinking an eye. But a measly bandit? No, you couldn't finish him. You made me do it. And I died."

Behind him, as if through a mist, Brayden could see the shapes of the other crew members appear, trudging towards them. "We all died," Reynard continued. "How ironic. You were the one meant to disappear, no one else, and now we're all gone."

Brayden raised the knife between him and the ghosts, staggering back. He bumped into something, and jumped away, spinning to see what it was.

The bandit leader stood there, a sword as large as himself held over his head.

The leader laughed. "I should have just killed you. You're a worthless brat. Your father's too busy to ransom you, anyway. After all, you're only good at getting the people around you killed. But you live on, useless as ever."

From his right, Reynard lunged forward, his sword plunging towards the boy. The bandit's huge sword swung down. Brayden stumbled back and fell. As his head struck against the ground, he saw the giant sword cleave through Reynard, who collapsed on Brayden.

He jerked awake, sweat streaming from his brow. He blinked at the bright sunlight that came through the window. Pushing back his blankets, he sat up and took in his surroundings.

The previous day he'd traveled late into the night, finally reaching Coricstead well past midnight. He'd been greeted by a shocked servant, who ran to get Mason. Brayden had expected the chamberlain to insist on waking his parents, but instead Mason had taken one look and ordered him to bed.

The soft mattress and thick blankets had swallowed him up and pulled him straight to a deep slumber.

Deep until the nightmare.

He rubbed his eyes, breaking free some of the bits of sand that had crusted around them. Slowly he stood and went to the water basin to wash the rest of the sweat and sand from his face.

"I suppose nightmares are to be expected," he said, staring at his rippling reflection in the water. He shuddered, remembering the still forms of Reynard, the assassin, and the other crew members. *It's not your fault any of them died,* Brayden told himself, but the icy horror lingered in his chest.

He turned away and went to work pulling on fresh clothes. The cloth felt soft and airy against his skin, like velvet compared to his stained and torn travel clothes.

One glance outside told him it was past noon. His stomach rumbled. He grabbed a brush to fix his hair. Before he could eat, he needed to seek audience of the king.

Bracing himself, he opened the door and exited to the hall.

And was pulled into a crushing hug. Pain stabbed him, and he failed to choke back a yelp.

"Are you okay?" said Tyler, releasing Brayden and taking a step back.

Grinning through the burning pain in his ribcage, Brayden leaned against the door way. "Of course," he said. "I was surprised is all. That, and you sometimes forget your own strength." If Tyler knew about the bandits, he'd never let Brayden out of the castle again.

"Why'd you sleep so long?" Tyler asked. "I've been worried sick about you. You should have returned ages ago."

"Tyler, how long have you been waiting out here for me?" asked Brayden, glad his brother had accepted his explanation.

A servant had also been waiting outside his door, but the man merely bobbed a quick bow before dashing down the hall. No doubt to tell the chamberlain Brayden was awake.

"Mason told us before breakfast that you'd come back. Mother said to let you sleep, but I couldn't spend my day wondering if you were awake yet."

"You did at least finish breakfast, right?" Brayden narrowed his eyes. "It's lunchtime."

"Enough about me. What happened to you? You were gone so long."

Brayden sighed. "Can *I* at least get something to eat," he asked, "regardless of your bad habits?"

"Of course, you must be starved, and Father will be busy with court matters right now. Mason told the kitchen staff to keep something warm for you."

In the kitchen, Brayden found a delicious meal, the first warm breakfast he'd had since leaving Chris's group. He ate quickly and downed two cups of milk before Mason himself arrived.

"I hope you're well rested from your travels?" he said.

"Yes. Thank you for letting me be," Brayden said with a smile. Though the man often irritated him, he'd missed Mason.

"Anyone could see you were about to collapse last night, and it was your mother who insisted that we not wake you this morning," he said. "But, now that you're awake, your parents would like to see both of you. In the Stone room," he added.

"The Stone room?" Brayden asked, raising an eyebrow. He knew he'd been recalled because of the Shards being stolen, but it still seemed an odd place to meet.

"There's something that Father didn't mention in the letter," whispered Tyler. "You'll see."

Tyler set a brisk pace as they went to a little-traveled corner of the castle, inconveniently at the opposite end from the kitchens, and up several stories. Finally they reached an old oaken door, large and heavy, with an ornate keyhole beneath the bronze handle.

Tyler knocked, and Brayden recognized the muffled voice of his father telling them to enter.

Both his father and mother were there, and one of the Shard caretakers. The last of these was surprising, but Brayden's gaze went to the right where there was a large glass wall—which he knew to be magically reinforced—through which he could see the Riddled Stone, resting on a pedestal.

Only the Stone was different. Normally it gleamed white, but now a black substance that reminded him of moss covered it.

"Brayden. Welcome home, son," his father said. "I'm glad you are well. We've been worried."

"I'm glad to be home," he said. For a second he hesitated, then asked, "What's wrong with the Stone?"

"Straight to the point," said the king with a slight smile. "Unfortunately we don't know. There's no record of this ever happening before. We would let the caretaker in to examine it, except we don't have the Shards."

Brayden's eyes shifted to the large stone door that led through the glass to the room where the Stone rested. Carved in the door was a hollow, designed to fit the five Shards, arranged in a sphere as they would have been around the Stone, before King Miles had touched them.

The Stone itself powered the magic guarding it, making the door the only way in and the five Shards together the only key.

Brayden swallowed.

"I need not tell you why we're so concerned," said the king. "Without getting inside, we have no way to figure out if the Stone is simply dying or is being sabotaged. If it's the latter, it could become dangerous. While you were in South Raec was there any sign they might be causing this, to weaken us before starting a war?"

Brayden's thoughts went straight to the assassin, and he nearly shuddered.

Then he thought of Chris Fredrico. There was no way he should know that the Shards were the key to the Stone, but it seemed suspicious that he was still in the country. And if another Shard had been stolen…

He remembered Arnold's voice, almost begging him to understand: "Even the king might make a mistake."

They had saved his life. Surely that earned them some benefit of doubt.

Biting the inside of his lip, Brayden shook his head.

"No, nothing happened in South Raec to make me believe they were seeking war. King Orin could not find anything related to the attack on the merchants, but he cooperated fully. He even wanted to write up a new, stronger peace treaty. A few younger lords showed prejudice against the ambassador and myself, but none of them struck me as the plotting type."

$\text{\small ❧} 27 \text{\small ❧}$

Brayden

After the meeting was over, the king and Tyler had gone to the audience chamber. The queen accompanied Brayden as he returned to his room. As they strolled back through the halls, his mother filled him in on what had changed in the castle since he left. He nodded and smiled at the appropriate moments, though he only half listened.

"You've grown up so much. I wish you'd notice it," said the queen, squeezing Brayden's shoulder and finally drawing his attention.

"You're just saying that. I'm still clumsy, and politics goes over my head," Brayden said, shaking his head.

"You might not have noticed, but when the king summoned you to the court, you did just fine. And from the reports the ambassador sent us, it sounds like you helped out."

"Really? I'm pretty sure he hated me by the end of day two. He was practically jumping with glee when Father sent the letter to recall me."

"The report may have had some bias in its tone, but he's a professional. He related the events accurately."

"Mother, I think you're just as biased, if in the other way," said Brayden.

She laughed. Brayden couldn't help a smile, but it vanished quickly.

His mother tilted her head towards him, her deep blue eyes narrowing. They walked in silence for a minute. Then her hand shot out to tousle his hair.

"Hey!" he said, ducking away. He glowered at her as he patted his hair smooth again. "What was that for?"

"Something's been on your mind since earlier. What is it?" she asked. "You can talk to me, Brayden."

"It's nothing," said Brayden.

"You know, it's not wise to lie to your mother," she said, smirking. "Mothers get a sixth sense when it comes to their children."

Brayden bit his lip. It would be nice to talk to someone about everything that had happened since he left the capital.

"If..." he began, faltering. "If I were to see something that would cause most people to jump to a conclusion, a logical conclusion, but to act on it would have bad consequences. Even if I don't have an alternate interpretation, and not acting could also have bad consequences— Is it right to wait to tell others what I saw, in hopes of finding another explanation?"

The queen stopped, a frown wrinkling her brow. "Well, that is a peculiar situation. How much worse would the wrong reaction be, compared to not acting at all?"

Brayden gnawed the inside of his cheek. As far as being attacked by an assassin went, then it was a case of possibly avoiding a war, versus starting a war for sure. Unless it *was* South Raec behind the attempt, and King Orin had fooled him, and now they might attack preemptively. His eyes widened, considering how many might die if he didn't report.

And what about Chris? The man had defied the king's law. But was he dangerous?

"But you also have to compare the best cases," his mother added, taking his hand and squeezing it. "With any decision, there's a careful balance between what could go right and what could go wrong. Sometimes we have to take risks to get the preferred results."

Brayden looked at her, his brows furrowed. "That's not helpful. How am I supposed to know when to take a risk and when to play safe? People— What if people's lives depended on my decision?"

His mother laughed again, the sound like musical bells filling the hall.

"Mother, this is important," Brayden said. The corners of his lips twitched as he resisted the temptation to laugh with her.

"I'm sorry," she said, wiping a tear from the corner of her eye. "It's just, you summed up what it's like to be king so perfectly. Almost every choice your father makes affects his people in some way or another. Maybe not to the extent of life and death, but their livelihood and comfort. Even decisions that don't affect them directly often have aftereffects that can't be predicted."

"Father's the king. He's always been king, or at least known he would be," said Brayden. "But how do *I* make a decision like that?"

"Son, these types of decisions don't get easier with experience. Some people have a talent for them, and some people don't, but nobody finds them easy. At least, no one who has a heart."

His mother sighed and shook her head. "The only thing you, or your father, can do in these situations is go by your gut. You were the one who saw what happened, so you're the one who can judge best what it means."

Brayden had no idea why Chris would still be in North Raec unless he was stealing the Shards, but his gut told him that Chris and his friends weren't planning anything treasonous.

"But." His mother turned Brayden to face her, gripping both of his shoulders. "As far as people jumping to conclusions go, perhaps you should give those people more credit. It's up to you, of course, and I trust your judgment, but carrying burdens alone only makes them heavier. And those people have been making decisions like this far longer than you."

That'd be great, if those people thought much of my opinion—or gut feeling, in this case, he thought.

"But of course, this is all hypothetical," said his mother, winking at him. "Since if you'd actually seen something that important, and hadn't told the king, you'd be in quite a bit of trouble."

Brayden reddened. "I— But—"

"Shh," she pressed her finger to her lips. "I won't tell on you. After all, this conversation was a theoretical discussion. In case you ever do come into this sort of situation."

"Right," said Brayden. "Thanks, Mother."

Her eyes narrowed. "But your decision had better be right. You might not be the king, or even the crown prince, but you still have a responsibility to our people."

Brayden grimaced. This conversation kept confusing him again, just as he thought he understood.

"Now, we were going somewhere," she said, turning down a hall. "You room is this way, right?"

"Wait," said Brayden.

She looked back, raising an eyebrow at him.

"I think I'd like to go to the library." Perhaps something there would help him understand what was going on.

They had only gone a few steps when a tall, slender woman appeared. Her blond braid was interwoven with pearls. More pearls adorned her neck, and seed pearls sparkled in the lace of her shimmery, pale pink gown. She looked familiar to Brayden, but he couldn't quite place her face.

The woman dropped a deep curtsy. "Queen Jennifer, Prince Brayden. It is a pleasure to meet you."

The queen bowed her head gracefully, so Brayden gave the woman a half bow.

"Ambassador Joline. I trust you are well today?" Brayden's mother said.

She'd seamlessly switched to queen mode in a way that made Brayden jealous. He didn't even have a prince mode. Instead, he folded his hands behind his back, standing at attention in the one position that guaranteed he wouldn't do something clumsy and embarrassing. Assuming he could hold still for the whole conversation.

"I feel excellent today," said Joline, beaming at the queen. "And you, young prince? You look to be in good health. I hope your trip to South Raec was uneventful?" Joline lowered her eyes. "I hate the thought that the two Raecs would go to war yet again."

"It was, thank you," said Brayden. He supposed such questions were to be expected. But it still made him feel uncomfortable, knowing what had happened.

Joline clasped her hands together, her beam returning. "Fantastic. That's so wonderful to hear."

"Lady Joline," said the queen. "My son has only just returned this morning and needs his rest. Would you keep me company while I take a turn in the garden?"

Joline gasped. "How thoughtless of me. He must be exhausted. The garden would be delightful. It was a pleasure to talk with you,

Prince Brayden." She dropped a swift curtsy.

Brayden returned a slight bow. "The pleasure was mine."

He sighed with relief as the two women disappeared around the corner. Then he continued on his way to the library.

☙ 28 ❧

Terrin

> "South of where thy enemies dwell,
> Where traitors plot of evil deeds,
> You'll find the fifth guardian.
> Fear his paws, his claws are sharp,
> He roams where man is feared to go.
> In the open you'll find that he defends
> Where next your journey takes you."

Terrin shuddered. Chris spoke in a trance-like way, as he always did when he recited the riddles. It was just one more reason for her to distrust the magic that surrounded the Riddled Stone and everything involved with it. But she'd already decided to follow this quest through, no matter what.

"That doesn't make sense," said Thomas, his brow furrowed. His eyes crossed—Terrin had noticed they did that when he was in deep thought.

They had left the lighthouse an hour ago. Now, back on the expanse of the moor, they'd stopped to eat a simple lunch and discuss the riddle.

"The enemy must be South Raec," Thomas continued, "but the next riddle can't be there. Even if the Riddled Stone wasn't a North Raecan relic, there's no way King Miles could have traveled to the South and back."

Chris shook his head. "I don't think South Raec is the enemy in the riddle. I think—" he paused, his fingers rubbing his beard. "I think it's Duke Grith."

"What?" exclaimed Thomas.

Terrin raised her eyebrow, and Nora tilted her head. Arnold only pursed his lips.

"How is Duke Grith an enemy of anybody?" Thomas asked. "Least of all Miles."

"First off," Chris said, "I don't think the riddles we're reading are the same as the ones Miles would have read. After all, you said Miles was a farmer. The clues we've been able to figure out weren't things a farmer would have known. For instance, only Terrin knew the swamp song."

Terrin nodded. "Very few people would have recognized that. And Miles only traveled with his sister and a friend. And traveling during the war would have made them as wary of people as we are, to avoid being labeled as deserters."

"Wait," said Arnold. "I thought Miles traveled alone?"

Chris raised an eyebrow. "Was that in one of your dreams?" he asked.

"Yes," said Terrin, realizing she'd never told him that last dream. She had awakened in the grasp of Ceianna's grandmother and her wraiths, and then there was the battle, and running from the soldiers. After that, the dream hadn't seemed important.

"Wait, Terrin had the dreams?" Arnold asked. "The same dreams you had?"

"I suppose we didn't mention that," said Chris. "I'd forgotten that only Nora and I were awake. It was right before we left the swamp, and then everything went crazy, and I forgot to tell you guys."

Terrin shuddered at the memory of that night. Because of the dreams, she had almost thrown herself off their raft and drowned. She was glad to be rid of them.

"I stopped having the dreams just after we separated," Chris continued. "And Terrin had them instead. I had told Nora to tell me if she had them, but you two were asleep. Have either of you had dreams?"

"Yes, actually," Arnold said. "I didn't think much of it, since I assumed the dreams were your thing, Chris. Like the riddles. And my dreams didn't make much sense. But, yes."

"What were they about?"

"Well, there was a weird one about Duke Grith. He was in Coricstead, and there was someone else there who knew we were going to the cliffs. And the guy who was spying on us had a weird glowing stone. I've been watching for anyone following us, though, and I haven't seen anyone."

Thomas stared at Arnold. "You… what? But why would Duke Grith be spying on us?"

"I had a dream about Duke Grith before," Chris said. "He was recruiting my older brother Anthony to help him with something that sounded a lot like treason."

Arnold huffed. "I should have known someone who boasts that much about knighthood couldn't be trusted."

Terrin almost grinned. Arnold had always resented his older cousin. "I bet Anthony was the one who framed you for stealing the Shard, Chris," she said.

"But why?" asked Nora. "What would Duke Grith need the

Shards for?"

"He used magic," said Chris. "In the dream. Maybe he thinks he's powerful enough to use the Shards for something."

Terrin laughed. "I hope he does, and they burn out his magic. It would serve him right."

"No doubt. But for now, our main concern is the riddle. We'll worry about the duke later," said Chris. "If he is our enemy, then the next riddle must be somewhere south of Charlon. Thomas, can you think of anything? You come from Charlon, don't you?"

Thomas ran his fingers through his hair. "The Dragon's Teeth hills. It's said that in ancient times there was a great city in that area. But it was destroyed, and now the hills are haunted by the ghosts of the fallen. It's not as dreaded as the Dark Forest, or even the swamp, but people avoid traveling there."

"Sounds like a place to start," said Chris.

"What I want to know," said Terrin, crossing her arms, "is what this 'fifth guardian' thing is about."

"Well, it is the fifth riddle," said Thomas. "I suppose the riddles are in a way guardians of the Riddled Stone, or at least were."

"But so far, they haven't had paws or claws," said Nora.

"They have had guardians though," said Chris. "Think about the eagle earlier? And the tree guarded the one in the swamp."

"And the wraiths," added Terrin. "Or at least, Ceianna's grandmother was watching the tree. I think watching over the tree might have passed through her family, the same way taking care of the wraiths did."

"How— Never mind," said Chris.

"What about the second riddle? Unless you saw something we didn't, there wasn't anything guarding it," said Arnold.

"There were the dolphin statues," said Chris. "They marked the pillar over the entrance to the riddle's cave. And the magic reacted when Thomas and I poked around them. And I don't think we need to question whether the first riddle had guardians," Chris finished.

"Well, I hope this guardian turns out more like the first two than the last two," said Nora, shivering.

No, not like the harpies, Terrin thought. *We got lucky there. If they had wanted us dead, we would be.*

"Well, there's another question for Thomas," said Chris. "What do you think the fifth guardian might be? Before, it's been related to the area, at least vaguely."

"The legends say a dragon destroyed the city."

"Perfect!" cheered Arnold. "I can finally fulfill my dream of defeating a dragon."

"I doubt that," drawled Terrin. "We have yet to run into anything mythical, and dragons still aren't real."

Thomas coughed and continued. "There are many animals native to that area. And if dolphins count as 'related to' a mountain lake, then who knows what counts for the hills? I will say that the line about defending doesn't sound like just a statue."

"No, it doesn't." Chris sighed. "One thing is for sure. When we reach the hills, we should go prepared."

"Well, I'll be sure to lend a hand to protect us," said Arnold. "Though it be my last."

Nora and Chris stifled giggles, but Terrin rolled her eyes. "Arnold, you're a pain."

Arnold laughed. "I try."

ᵔ 29 ᵔ

Trillory

Trill collapsed on the bed, staring at the floor where she'd spent the last eternity pacing. She thought she could see the beginning of a path being carved into the carpet.

She didn't know why, but the more she mulled it over, the more sure she was that Anthony was up to something. It was an irrational idea. Anthony had always been a stuck-up jerk. Why should he be up to anything more now?

But she hadn't been able to shake the feeling. Especially after the way he'd oh-so-casually mentioned that Duke Grith would be back soon. Why would he know that when the duke hadn't sent notice to Eric or anyone in the manor?

She sighed. Sitting here wasn't going to get her anywhere but insanity, and Eric was hung up in the audience chamber. She needed to go somewhere. Pulling on simple, soft-soled court shoes, she left the room and started wandering. Though she was searching for something new to distract her, she drifted towards the north wing out of habit. Irritated, she turned down a branch of halls in the opposite direction.

At home, this sort of mood would send her to the library. Reading always helped. It occurred to her that she might be able to unlock the magic room and find a book to read. Eric wouldn't mind. Rather, he'd be pleased if she could figure out a specific spell like that on her own.

She stopped, mapping out the most direct route to the north wing. Then she jogged back towards the more major halls of the castle, stopping cold when she heard the tap, tap of boots on stones.

She didn't know why, but her whole body went tense, her instincts telling her to flee.

Don't be ridiculous, there's no reason I shouldn't be here, she told herself.

Still, she couldn't help backtracking around the last turn she'd made.

She pressed herself against the wall, listening. The footsteps rounded the corner up ahead and started fading away. She peeked around the corner.

To her surprise, it was Anthony. He walked briskly, and as he passed another turn, he glanced around, making her retreat back out of sight.

If she had no reason to be in this part of the castle, Anthony had less. He was social, and she'd never seen him try to avoid people. And, as far as she knew, he didn't know about Duke Grith's or Eric's magical habits.

Leaning back out, she waited until he turned a corner, then quietly dashed down the hall after him. She kept her body low and her steps light, thankful she'd chosen quiet shoes.

When she reached the turn he'd taken, she stopped and leaned out, just in time to see his next turn.

She followed him like this through the upper north wing until he'd reached a dead end. She frowned, more confused than ever as he started down the last hall. The rooms here were unused, especially now with the manor down to a skeleton inhabitance.

He stopped and faced the wall between two alcoves, and then he glanced around. Trill tensed, as it was too late for her to duck back. But he seemed to miss the couple inches of her head sticking out below waist level. She silently sighed with relief.

He turned back and pulled a necklace out from around his neck, and held it up, muttering some words she couldn't make out. Magic burst from the necklace, swirling through the air in two tendrils. The first touched the wall, which seemed to set it a-tingle with more magic. The second tendril wrapped itself around Anthony's head.

A shudder ran through Anthony's body. Then he pushed against the wall and disappeared through it.

Trill's mouth dropped open.

Obviously the wall itself was an illusion, but why? And what would Anthony be using a passage for?

Keeping low to the ground, she crept towards the wall. The magic from the charm, at least she assumed it was a charm, still hung in the air, but was evaporating quickly. The magic of the wall was still there, but faint.

It would be easy to tear through the illusion of the wall, but she wouldn't have the first clue of how to fix it afterward. Instead, she reached for the remains of the charm. She should be able to mimic it, and that wouldn't leave traces.

She shut her eyes, letting her own magic drip from her fingers and out to touch the already-cast magic. It spread, molding itself to the same shape and pattern. Adding more power, Trill let it expand to encircle her face and then towards the wall.

She opened her eyes. In place of the stone wall, she saw a plain, oaken door. Gingerly she pressed her ear against it, listening for Anthony's foot falls. They were difficult to hear through the door, but they were still there, if faint.

She waited until they were gone, then gently pushed the door open. She was relieved to find the hinges well-greased. Beyond it was a spiraling staircase, lit by torches of magical flame. The flames were dying, though, and she guessed they'd been lit by Anthony's passing, perhaps by the same charm that let him through the door.

She shut the door behind her and started down the stairs, keeping one hand against the wall, trying to look around the spiral as she followed it.

A few minutes later, she reached the bottom. She shivered. This must be the dungeon level of the castle. She'd never been in Charlon Manor's dungeon, but she'd imagined them to be murky and damp like the Fredricburg mansion's. These, however, despite being carved straight out of the rock, were clean, and a slight breeze of fresh air came from somewhere.

Since the torches here seemed to be magical as well, she followed the brightest flames. She kept low and close to the wall. Though the flames made this no better for hiding than the center of the hall, it still felt safer.

Trill glanced down each side hall she passed. Doors lined both sides of the dark corridors, each with a small, barred window. After the third one, she gave in to curiosity and moved down one of the side halls. She pressed her ear against the first door, just to be sure it was empty, then peeked through its window. She couldn't see much, so she opened the door. It was a thick, heavy door. The wood was old, but still sturdy. The room beyond it was small, even sparser than the rooms of the north wing, with no natural light to brighten it up. A bare bed stood to the side, a cracked bowl sat on a small rickety table with a single chair. She checked the small chest at the foot of the bed and found nothing. She shut the door and checked two more identical rooms before returning to the main hall.

By then, the torches in the area had faded to embers. Bending down, she dashed after the lights.

Finally the lit torches took a turn. Trill slowed as she rounded the corner. The torches here were bright, and she was sure she'd caught up with Anthony.

This hall had fewer doors, but one near the end was open, and the gleam of torch light flooded from the room into the hall. She stopped just outside the room, crouched low to the ground, and peered around the corner.

Though her vision was limited, she could tell that this room was large enough to fit a conference table. Anthony stood with his back to the door, only a few yards away, his head turned to the side. Trill pulled back, trying to soften her breathing.

From further in the room, she could just hear the murmur of voices. After a minute, one voice became clear. A chill ran through her spine as she recognized it: Duke Grith.

"It appears the boy has not even reported the incident. Which means either the assassin backed out of the job, or the young prince is smarter than he looks."

"Brayden? Smart?" Anthony snorted. "Even if he somehow defeated the assassin on his own, he knows nothing of politics or people. He would have gone whining straight to my brother Gillian about it."

"Anthony, I think you assume too much. Have you ever had a full conversation with the prince? Or even met him? Just because he's done nothing worth mentioning, doesn't mean he lacks brains. Not that it matters. If the assassin's alive, I'll take care of him later.

We need to move to Plan B. Pity. It's a messy plan."

Trill pressed her hand to her mouth. She didn't have to understand what Grith and Anthony were talking about to know it was treasonous.

Grith continued, "How went it with the Shards?"

"The same as before." Anthony sighed.

"Bother. Not that it matters, it won't work without all of them. Still, Christopher had better come through."

Trill gasped, glad she'd already blocked her mouth. Her hands tightened into fists. Anger burned in her throat. Chris would never work with Anthony, treason or no.

Which meant they were using him.

And if they were using him, it was almost certain they had framed him.

"As a side note," the duke continued. "How has Eric done in my absence?"

"Excellent. Everyone seems pleased with his skills as an administrator."

"If only the same could be said of his magic. And how is your sister?"

Trill could hear the smile in Anthony's voice. "She and Eric have bonded, as I thought they would. Nigh inseparable, as far as I can tell. In fact, I wouldn't be surprised if he already knows about her magic."

"Good, good," said Grith. "Pity, though. I doubt he told her my natural ability."

"What?" said Anthony. "Why is that—"

"Haven't I told you? I can sense the presence of people around me."

Trill's heart jumped to her chest, and she stumbled backwards. Turning, she scrambled on all fours as she tried to run while pulling herself to her feet.

She felt the magic before it reached her, racing towards her like tentacles. She looked back, raising her arm to block it. Magic sprung from her hand, and the duke's magic bounced away.

He entered the hall and laughed. She continued to scoot away, but his magic was already returning, spread wider now, and stronger. She tried to stretch her shield, but the duke's magic broke through and wrapped around her. Her body froze.

"You are strong," said the duke. "But that magic was sloppy."

Anthony appeared from the room and gaped at her. "How—?"

"No doubt she followed you. Sneaky thing."

Trill glared at the duke. She thought about trying to break his magic, but she could feel its ironclad strength.

"Let me go," she said.

"I intend to," the duke said. "But I've been wanting to talk to you. I had planned to wait until after I'd taken the throne. But since you're here now, there's no time like the present."

"I have nothing to discuss with you," she snapped. "You're a traitor to your country."

"So narrowed-minded, Lady Trillory. I have only the best of intentions for my country. I will make us strong once more, something the Coric dynasty cannot do. And I'd like your help with that. You see, Eric's magic is forever limited by his inability to focus it."

The Duke crouched to look her in the eyes.

"But you and I are different. We have power *and* focus. We are special. I think you already have begun to understand how magic really works. Those rules you read in books, they don't apply to me. I can break them, and I believe you can, too. If you will let me teach you."

"You're evil," Trill glowered.

"Yes, well, this little misunderstanding was why I meant to put our conversation off." Grith sighed and stood. "I'm sure you'll come around, though. Anthony, would you accompany your sister to her room? I have business to take care of, but I'm sure it won't take long."

"Won't she just escape?" asked Anthony. "You said yourself that she has magic, so just locking the door won't do much."

"Oh, my binding spell should last long enough to take care of any escape plans she might make. Just watch her until I come."

The duke paused, smirking at Trill.

"And if you're worried about her talking to someone, you shouldn't be. Who could she tell? Eric?" He laughed. "You've said yourself she's a recluse with no other friends."

❧ 30 ❧

Brayden

Dust exploded in Brayden's face as he slammed the book shut. Coughing, he staggered back to the bookshelf and slid the book into place.

In the weeks of reading every history and politics book the king's family owned, he had discovered two things. One was that these books were not read very often.

The second was that his Coric ancestors had a tendency towards war. Rash decisions leading to disaster filled his family history.

So far they'd avoided this war. The king had told the ambassador to open a discussion with King Orin about the new treaty. Not because of Brayden's advice, but after seeking Duke Grith's opinion.

But the last of the Shards had disappeared. It hadn't been stolen, exactly. The caretaker had been watching it one moment, and the next it was gone.

And, each day, Brayden went to check on the Riddled Stone. It was only getting worse. The white surface was completely covered now, not even a glimmer of light shining through.

He grabbed another book off the shelf and turned back to his chair. He wasn't sure what he was looking for anymore, but he felt that reading was the closest he could come to helping. Perhaps it didn't matter, and they'd never understand the Stone.

As long as the war didn't start, that would be good enough for him.

He curled on the chair and opened the book, dust showering into his lap, and read. It was just a rehash of stuff he'd read before. Miles Coric found the Stone by following riddles, and then he returned to the army and, using the Stone's power, rallied them and chased the South Raecan army from their land.

Brayden yawned. His eyelids drooped.

He stood in the Stone room, inside the glass chamber, but a perfectly round obsidian-like shell covered the Stone. He reached out and touched it. The next thing he knew, he was standing in a cave. The black rock shattered, falling away in five Shards, and there was the Stone, gleaming a blinding white.

He blinked away the tears and found himself back in the library. The book had slid from his fingers and fallen open against his chest. He sat up and shut the book, placing it in his lap and folding his hands. Then he leaned back and stared across the room.

The Stone was reverting.

The Stone's shell was closing up, in preparation to pick a new master.

Perhaps no one had stolen the Shards. They'd just disappeared to reappear on the Stone. Maybe the Stone itself would disappear in time, returning to where it was found, and some other adventurer would happen upon the riddles and find it and be chosen.

Someone like Christopher Fredrico.

There were parallels. Miles had escaped a losing battle, leaving the army to take his sister to safety. According to the record, he meant to return, but he'd discovered the riddles, at which point he'd set off wandering cross-country. He was labeled a deserter, a traitor to his king.

Chris was also considered a traitor, yet he remained in North Raec. Perhaps because he, too, was wandering around, following riddles?

Brayden bit his lip. That seemed plausible, but why was the Stone selecting a new master now?

In Miles's case, the old royal family had died before he arrived at the battle. The Stone had seemingly awoken in a time of need, to choose the new king.

Was the Coric line going to die? How? And why now, after they avoided the war?

He stood, dropping the book to the table, and exited the library.

Without thinking, he went straight to the audience chamber, realizing too late that he shouldn't be there. He hesitated outside the door and turned away. His first instinct had been to talk to his father, but what good would that do?

"Hi, Dad, I think our entire family might die somehow." Like that wouldn't be an awkward opening.

A horn blew from the audience chamber. He jumped half out of his skin, then turned back. He stopped outside the audience chamber to listen, though the footman guarding the door cast him a weird look.

"A messenger fro—" the other footman tried to announce, but someone else cut him off.

"My king, I bear ill news for you, from the king of South Raec."

Brayden peeked around the corner to see the messenger, half

collapsed on the ground, gasping for breath and holding up a scroll, letting it roll open.

"A declaration of war."

He clapped his hand to his mouth and stepped back. Impossible. King Orin wouldn't just declare war for no reason like this.

From the hall, there was an uproar of boots striking the ground as people jumped to their feet and started shouting.

"Silence!" Father commanded.

The voices hushed.

"Let me see that."

No one spoke for several minutes.

"It would appear," the king began, pain evident in his voice, "that the South never wanted peace. Send word that all nobles are to prepare their knights at once."

The Stone knew. It knew war was coming, thought Brayden. *But… does this really mean that my family will die, and Chris will take their place? Does Chris know that's what's happening?*

Brayden's hands tightened to fists. He didn't care how the Stone acted. He would make sure that his father and Tyler stayed safe, no matter what.

❧ 31 ❧

Christopher

Cupping his hands in the cool stream, Chris splashed his face. It was truly summer now. Even though they'd been riding day after day for weeks, he still found himself sweating profusely within an hour of starting. Picking up the water skin he'd been filling, he swung it over his shoulder as he stood. He stretched his legs and then turned back to where Thomas was preparing lunch.

He noticed Arnold pulling out the wooden practice swords for him and Nora.

"Don't mock fight today," Chris called. "We'll reach the hills soon, and I want you in top shape when we find the riddle. Just in case those lines about the guardian meant more than a statue."

"Aw," said Arnold. "I was in the mood for a good spar."

"What, aren't you always excited for a chance to nap?" asked Terrin. She had pulled out her bow string. She looped it over one end of the bow, then hooked that end around her ankle, pushing both ends together with ease to stretch the string across.

"I still prefer dueling," said Arnold. "Though naps are a close second."

"Going hunting again today?" asked Chris, looking at Terrin's bow. "We have enough meat to last a while."

"And we can always use more. And who knows how long we'll be in the hills, or where we'll go next."

Hopefully home, thought Chris, glancing north. It was a week's hard ride, but he knew that Fredricburg was there. Months had passed since he left his city, and the desire to see his sister clawed at his chest. And to relax in the school library, reading about adventures instead of having them.

But not until he completed this quest. And that was assuming he could prove his innocence.

A couple hours later, on horseback once more, they entered the hills. Terrin's hunting trip had gained two squirrels for their food supply. Arnold had indeed slept the entire time, even while Chris played on the flute Nora had given him.

As they carved their way through the hills, Chris couldn't keep his skin from crawling. Usually only Terrin could sense magic, but here he felt wisps of something floating through the air. No doubt the source of the ghost stories. The hills shot up on either side, the triangular granite outcroppings scattered across them looked like miniature mountains—or maybe teeth. Huge pines studded the hillside wherever the ground evened out.

He saw movement in the corner of his eye and spun in the saddle. Arnold glanced up from his arm which he'd been flexing. At Chris's suggestion, Arnold had put his prosthetic and shield on when they mounted up.

"What?" asked Arnold.

"Sorry, just… would you stop fidgeting with that?"

"I don't mean to, but it's uncomfortable. I don't like this hand."

"It's the closest you'll get to the real thing," said Thomas. "You have to get used to it, if you want to use that shield."

"I know," said Arnold, "But it feels like there ought to be a better option. A quicker one, at least. I'm supposed to rush into battle. I can't do that if I'm fighting with my own arm. And I won't always be forewarned."

"Shh," hissed Terrin.

The group fell silent, pulling their horses to a stop. Chris strained his ears, wondering what the forest girl's sharper ears had picked up, but he couldn't make out anything. He raised an eyebrow at Terrin, but she held her finger to her lips.

For a minute they stood there, Chris tense with anticipation. Then Terrin shook her head. "It's gone. I think I heard something growling."

"Are you sure you didn't just want me to shut up?" asked Arnold.

"Yes," said Terrin. "Chris, we should try to find some high ground. Scope out the area."

He nodded and nudged Marc back to a walk, looking for an easy way up the hill to their right.

After several minutes, they reached the top. The view revealed little. The Dragon's Teeth hills here were close together, rising as fast as they fell. To the north they dropped away, and Chris could make out a narrow woodland, and past that the gray smudge of Charlon.

"The magic is strongest over there," said Terrin, pointing southward.

Arnold stood in his saddle as he followed Terrin's gesture. "I wonder why this whole area feels magical," he said. "The other riddles didn't have this large a range."

"The others were enclosed," Chris pointed out. "This one could be in the open."

"And I don't think we're far from the source," said Terrin. "Though it's hard to tell where it is, exactly. We should get moving, though. Who knows how long it'll take to find it."

Chris nodded. "All right. Everyone grab a drink or snack, if you want it, then we're moving."

❧

Nora

Nora gathered her hair, trying to peel it off the back of her neck. She'd never liked putting her hair up, but today she felt jealous of Terrin's braid. The hills blocked any breeze that had made the heat bearable before.

"We're here," said Terrin up ahead, pointing to the next bend.

They rode single file, and Chris disappeared around the turn first. It took a minute for Nora, at the back of the line, to catch up. The gully between the hills opened dramatically, revealing an old, moss-covered pavilion. Some of the roof remained, supported by columns as thick as trees. But the stone blocks were crumbling, and one column had been reduced to a pile of rubble.

From the middle rose a rock pillar, like the other riddles, though Nora couldn't see any of the strange runes. Perhaps on the far side?

"I don't see a guardian," said Chris, his hand falling to his sword.

"Let's just get the riddle and get out," said Terrin.

Chris nodded and dismounted.

A roar echoed into the gully, vibrating off the hills. Terrin's horse Leaf cried out, skittering sideways.

Minty's body tensed, but Nora held her steady, directing her to pivot so Nora could search for the source of the roar. She'd just turned when a great brown bear rose up beside her, its paws as big as her head. Minty jumped sideways, tripped on some rubble and fell.

"Nora, jump free!" shouted Chris.

Too late. Nora's head struck the stone edge of the platform, and she lay still, one leg pinned beneath her horse. Her head throbbed, her vision hazy.

She saw someone moving between her and the bear. The whole world was sliding apart to make two equally blurry versions. She blinked, struggling to see clearly. She could make out the bear swinging its paw, knocking the person aside with a roar. Minty was trying to scramble to her feet, but the bear knocked her back down.

Minty screamed, and Nora winced. If she could brace herself against the horse, she might pull her leg out. She still felt numb from the fall, but she reached out, trying to find Minty's shoulder with her hand.

She felt the bear leaning over her, its hot breath against her cheek.

Then there was a yell, and the bear staggered away. This time Nora could tell the blur was Arnold by the round thing on his arm. He bounced back from the bear, and Nora guessed he'd just barreled straight into the thing.

The bear swung its paw and struck the shield. Its claws ripped straight through the cloth and against the metal with a screech that stabbed through Nora's head, sharp as an arrow.

Her vision was sliding back into place, but a blue film spread over the scene, making it even harder to see. She reached out for anything to grasp onto. Her fingers found the ridge between two pavilion stones, and she tried to pull her way free. She winced in pain, her leg unwilling to move. The stone broke from the pavilion.

She collapsed, blinded by blue now, her head thick with pain.

Then Chris's voice was in her ear, whispering far too loudly, "Hold still. You'll be okay."

She smiled and tried to nod. A hand squeezed her shoulder. The blue faded, and her entire body relaxed, exhaustion flooding over her.

෪ 32 ෪

Terrin

Terrin's fingers slid from the string, and the arrow flew free, striking the bear beneath its upraised arm. It howled, collapsing back to all fours and snapping the arrow in two.

Arnold jumped forward, his sword slashing across the monster's face. A streak of blood appeared, and the bear retreated, tossing its head. One paw shot out blindly, striking Arnold's shield.

He staggered under the blow, but stabbed the inside of its leg.

Terrin drew and released another arrow, this one aimed for its neck. It only clipped the beast. She grimaced.

She started to draw another arrow, but Minty finally clambered to her feet, pushed by Chris and Thomas, and blocked her shot. Thomas caught the horse's bridle and pulled her away from the fight, while Chris bent to scoop up Nora.

Terrin's heart skipped a beat as she saw how limp Nora was. Blood oozed from a gash on her head.

Averting her eyes from the blood, she clenched her jaw and drew the string.

"I'm not missing this time," she muttered as she aimed once more for the bear's neck. The bear roared, then rose back to a full stance, throwing off her aim.

Arnold took a step back, raising his shield.

She adjusted her aim, took a deep breath, and let the arrow fly. It struck straight through the bear's neck. The creature gave a gargled roar, staggering where it stood.

Arnold leaped forward, catching its body against his shield and shoving the bear sideways. It fell, and he spun with it, pulling his shield back to put his full weight into stabbing its heart, dropping to one leg as he did so.

Arnold froze, and Terrin half-lowered her bow, watching the bear. Then Arnold jumped back, leaving his sword behind, and called out, "Is Nora okay?"

Terrin turned to see where Thomas and Chris knelt over the girl. She lay on the open ground with a bedroll tucked under her head.

"She's fainted, and probably has a concussion," said Thomas.

"Is that thing dead?" Chris asked without looking up from Nora.

"Yes," said Arnold.

"Arnold, take Rich and look for the other horses," Chris said. All except the trained warhorse had panicked when the bear appeared. "Terrin, do what you can for Minty until Thomas has bandaged Nora."

"And I should take a look at you," said Thomas, glancing at Chris. "You took quite a blow there."

"I'm just bruised," Chris muttered. "I'll be fine."

Terrin turned to Minty, but paused, noticing the stone that Nora had torn free. She knelt and lifted it. Gasping at its weight, she dropped it again.

"Nora's stronger than I thought," she said.

"Adrenaline," said Thomas. "Good thing these stones are falling apart, or she could have dislocated her hip."

ᥰ

The heat faded as the sun sank behind the hills, casting shadows over the gully. Terrin sat at the edge of the pavilion, staring at the stone pillar in its center, her fingers drumming against her knee. The magic emanating from the rock felt crushingly heavy.

She heard Nora's small groan and was on her feet before Chris could say, "Nora's awake."

They all crowded around. Nora winced in pain and raised a hand to touch her bandaged forehead.

"How do you feel? Do you remember what happened?" asked Thomas.

Nora nodded, then grimaced.

"There was a bear," she said. "And Minty fell— Is Minty all right?" Nora tried to sit up, but sank back.

"She's fine," said Thomas. "I wouldn't ride her for a while, but she'll recover. Not that you'll be going far until that concussion's healed. Let me get you something for the pain."

Thomas stood and went to his bag.

"All that care for your horse, and you aren't going to show any worry for your hero?" said Arnold. "I'm starting to think you don't like me."

"What? No, I—" Nora stopped and narrowed her eyes at him.

"Just teasing you," Arnold said with a grin.

"Arnold, this isn't the time," said Terrin.

"What happened to the bear?" Nora asked, turning her gaze to Chris.

"It's dead," he said.

"And did you get the riddle?"

"Riddle?" Chris frowned. Then he laughed. "I forgot about it."

"Terrin," said Nora. "You should have reminded him."

"Now is hardly the time to worry about some ancient words scribbled on an old rock," Terrin said. "You could have died, you know."

"Not with you four looking after me."

"I'd rather wait until you're strong enough to at least stand before we think about the next riddle," said Chris. "It's not going anywhere, and, like Thomas said, neither are we."

"I'll be fine, once I have the pain medicine. You should read it before anything bad happens."

"Nothing bad will happen. We already defeated the bear," said Chris.

"Something bad always happens."

"Here, drink" said Thomas as he knelt beside Nora and handed her a cup.

With Thomas's help, Nora sat up and sipped at the herbs.

Terrin raised an eyebrow at Chris, crossing her arms. "She's right, you know. You should go look at the riddle. I'm not saying something else bad will happen, but there's still magic here. Remember how the tree attacked us?"

"Fine."

As Nora lay back down, Chris stood with a huff and approached the stone. Like the other riddle stones, it rose seamlessly from the ground, as if a part of the pavilion. Terrin had to wonder who—or what—had placed these things.

Chris circled the stone, then read aloud:

> "Flickering shadows linger,
> Clinging to a past long gone.
> Whispering of beauty lost,

Of truth that's been forgotten.
But death is all that remains,
Brought by fear and lies."

Before he finished, Terrin felt the magic bunch up. "Chris, move!" she shouted.

Without hesitation he dove off the pavilion. The others ducked.

Magic shot outward. The ground shook, and a thunderous crack echoed through the gully, followed by another.

Terrin looked up. One of the columns had fallen, taking half the remaining roof with it, and landed across the riddle pillar, smashing it. Chris lay inches away from the pile of rubble, covered in dust.

"That was close." Chris's words rattled as he stood and walked gingerly around the pavilion and back to the group.

They stared at the ruins in silence.

Then Arnold said, "You know, these things just get more and more cheerful, don't they?"

Chris shook his head, then flopped to the ground next to Nora. "But what does it mean?"

"Interesting," said Thomas. "Somewhere that used to be beautiful, but isn't."

"The shadows and truth sound like it has a history, probably a war. Ring any bells, Chris?" asked Terrin. Nora had been the best at history in school, but she needed to rest.

"Let me think." Chris rubbed his chin, but stopped and shook his hand. "Beards are weird," he muttered.

"I know where it is," said Nora. She winced as she propped herself up. "I didn't see any riddles there, but it matches perfectly."

"Where? Somewhere in the mountains?" asked Chris.

"No. In the Dark Forest."

"Nora, no one's been to the Dark Forest," said Terrin. She smiled, but the hair on the back of her neck prickled.

"I didn't mention it because—" Nora grimaced and pressed a hand to her forehead. "Reasons. I had reasons. But when we separated, and I lost Minty, she went to the Dark Forest. I went after her."

"You went into the Dark Forest and didn't die?" said Arnold. "What was it like?"

"It was… like the riddle." Nora shrugged.

"I think we should let her rest, and talk more tomorrow," said Thomas. "I'm as curious as the rest of you, but Nora's already pushing herself."

Nora met Chris's eyes, leaving it up to him whether she said more. He bit his lip. Then nodded.

"We should all sleep," he said.

ↂ 33 ↂ

Trillory

Trill awoke to the growling of her stomach. The fog in her head pounded against her skull with more strength than fog ought to have. She sat up, looking around her room.

It looked mostly as she'd left it. Her small writing desk to the left of her bed. The two cushioned seats shoved into the far corner, a dress draped across one. Her dresser opposite the desk, with washbowl and pitcher waiting, and next to that her closet. Someone had opened the folding doors to her balcony, though, and sunlight poured into the room, making her eyes water. She rubbed them and tried to shrug off the fatigue.

A metallic scrape at the door sent darts through her ears.

"What is it?" she called.

There was a click of the lock, and the door opened. Anthony entered, holding a tray with tea and scrambled eggs. "You're finally awake. Grith will be pleased. He was worried, you know," he said.

The sight of him banished the fog from her mind. She snatched up her pillow and flung it at him. He sidestepped it easily.

Trill regretted the action, as what energy she had went with the pillow, and she collapsed to the bed.

Anthony crossed the room and set down the tray.

"You poisoned me, didn't you?" she said, glaring up at him.

The last thing she remembered was a servant with a plate of food, noodles and a spicy sauce. And the pain that followed. Like her chest being ripped out through her mouth. She had no idea how much time had passed.

"Hardly. The duke and I still hope you'll see wisdom and join us. But for security, he had to remove your power. Grith explained to me that there's a very rare herb that nullifies magic. Not permanently, we're told."

She glanced at the new platter of food. "And there's more in that?"

"Yes, but don't worry. You only fell ill in the first place from the shock of losing your magic. That you're awake shows your body's adjusting. You should know, we've locked your door from the outside and told everyone you're sick, and contagious. You needn't worry about your social duties."

"Oh, joy." She rolled over, turning her back on him. "And what if I don't eat?"

"Then starve," Anthony snapped. "That will happen before the herbs lose effect, if that's what you're thinking."

Not that he'd care.

"Or," he added, in his honeyed court voice. "You could accept that Grith has won, swear allegiance to him, and go back to your nice, easy life."

"Go away already."

"Fine." Anthony took a deep breath. Then, in a more controlled tone, he said, "Take your time, Trill. The duke is willing to wait. Though you should know that Eric misses you."

The door slammed shut.

Trill crushed her bedsheets in her fist.

Eric.

How could he know what was going on and allow it?

Had everything been a trick from the beginning?

"Just wait, Anthony," she growled. "I'll escape. And when I do, everyone will see what you're really like."

♥

Arnold

Once more Arnold found himself floating in a castle, an eerily empty foyer this time. He turned and took a step back at the sight of Duke Grith standing beside a boy and a woman. It was a tapestry portrait, hanging above the duke's coat of arms.

"This must be Charlon," Arnold muttered. "Where our enemy dwells."

He turned and sped down the nearest hall and up a flight of steps. He didn't want to look at the face of a traitor to North Raec any longer than he had to.

He didn't count the number of corners he'd rounded before stopping to wonder at the quiet. Normally a manor this size had a bevy of servants scurrying here and there to keep the place squeaky clean.

Then he heard the thud of boots behind him. He spun just in time to see a young man run straight through him. He gasped, expecting pain, but felt only a brief icy cold.

Shivering, he turned to see the young man had stopped, turning back to stare at him. Arnold recognized him as an older version of the boy in the tapestry. Must be Grith's son. Eric, was it?

"Wha— No, not now," said the man. Then he turned and continued running.

Arnold floated after him, keeping up despite the break-neck speed.

Eric skidded to a stop in front of a door. With one hand he knocked, the other turning the handle.

"Locked, of course," he said, taking a step back.

He made a fist with his hand, staring at the lock.

Arnold leaned away. Did the man think he could punch it open?

Taking a deep breath, Eric made a movement like flinging something at the door. The handle exploded. The door swung open. He charged through.

"Eric? What the—?" Arnold recognized the voice. Trillory, Chris's twin sister. What was she doing here?

He darted into the room. He registered an ornate bed, fluttering curtains, some chairs and Trill standing on the balcony. A drizzling of rain had turned the sky gray.

"Trill, I'm so sorry. Magnolia told me everything," said Eric, moving towards her.

"Magnolia?" She frowned. "Wh— No, stay away." She held up her hands.

Eric paused. "Trill?"

"Don't call me that," she snapped. "You're not my friend. You tricked me, and I hate you."

"What? No, I didn't… Trill, I can explain."

He took another step forward and reached out to catch her hand.

"No," she said, and jerked away. She stumbled, struck against the balcony railing, and fell.

"Trillory!" shouted Arnold and Eric as one.

Arnold tried to run across the room. The pull of reality yanked him back to drag him from the dream. Fighting it felt like climbing a sand wall, but Arnold pushed himself forward.

Eric reached over the balcony railing, lunging after her and almost falling himself.

"Trill!" he shouted. His chin trembled.

Arnold leaned out, just for a second, and he saw her, three stories down, lying deathly still among the rose bushes. Then a whitish gray blur washed over his eyes, and he was back in camp.

"No!" he exclaimed, shooting up from his bedroll.

A gray, dreary light filled the clearing around the pavilion. He looked up and his heart rose to his throat. Rain clouds had gathered overhead.

There had been rain in the garden. And Trill—

"Arnold? What's wrong?" said Terrin, "Is it a dream?"

He jumped to his feet and dashed to Chris's side, kicking him in the shin.

"Ow!" said Chris, curling into a ball. "What was that for?"

"Wake up, everyone wake up." Arnold spun, looking for Thomas, but his bedroll was empty. "Where's Thomas?"

"He left just a second ago, to gather herbs. Arnold, what's wrong?" Terrin said.

"I'll get him. This is important, Trill's in trouble," Arnold called over his shoulder as he dashed down the path. "Thomas, wait. Come back."

He rounded a corner and skidded to a stop. A large hawk blocked the path in front of him, wings spread for flight. Its wide, gold eyes met his, and they stared at each other for a second, then the hawk sprang to the air and fled.

Shaking himself, Arnold dashed down the path to the next bend. The path stretched ahead a couple hundred feet before it vanished behind a rock tooth, but Thomas was nowhere to be seen.

"Thomas?" he called. "Come back!" he bit his lip. The old man shouldn't have gotten far, but Arnold didn't have time to search.

When he returned, Chris had woken Nora, and all three looked expectantly at him.

"Arnold, what do you mean Trill's in trouble?" asked Chris.

"I was in Charlon, at Grith's manor. And it was raining, and she was in her room, and she fell out the window."

"Arnold, slow down," Terrin said.

Arnold forced himself to take a deep breath and speak clearly. "I had another dream. I was in Charlon Manor. And Trill was there. It was raining, and she fell out a window, and I think she was dead."

All color drained from Chris's face, and his jaw dropped. "Bu— No!"

Arnold grabbed his shoulder and shook him. "Chris, don't zone out. It could happen any time. We have to hurry. We have to change the dream."

"What if we can't?" Chris met his eyes. "We couldn't change Terrin's dream, and—"

"Of course we can change it. What would be the dream's point, if we couldn't change it? We just didn't try hard enough with Terrin. We have to hurry, though."

"What about Thomas?" said Terrin.

"Nora's hurt. She can stay here and wait for him," said Arnold. He released Chris and grabbed his saddle.

"I'm not waiting here," said Nora. "We can leave a note for Thomas, but Trill's my friend, too. I can't stay here and worry about all of you."

"But, your head—" said Chris.

"I'm fine."

Chris bit his lip, then shook himself. "We don't have time to argue. Get your stuff. You can ride Thomas's horse."

❧ 34 ❧

Christopher

The first droplets of rain splattered against the pavement as they cantered into Charlon. The weather would chase most people inside, but it meant Arnold's dream could happen any minute. The remaining citizens shot them angry looks as they clattered by. One soldier yelled at them for reckless riding, but he didn't move from beneath the overhang of an inn's porch.

Up ahead Chris could see Grith's manor. He'd never been here before, but most manors had a side gate leading into the garden, rarely guarded except in wartime. The hard part would come once inside the castle.

They circled around to the east side of the manor and found a small side gate, more of a large door. He jumped from Marc's back and ran to the gate, flinging it open. Inside they found a narrow lane, just wide enough for a wagon. To their left ran the wall of a hedge maze. To their right, a shoulder-height stone wall separated them from the kitchen gardens.

"Let's find a place to leave the horses," said Chris as he shut the door behind them. "Nora, you'll stay with them. If anyone sees you, run. We'll meet up later, somehow."

"All right," Nora said.

They left their horses in the hedge maze. Chris led Terrin and Arnold back to the lane.

The stone wall opened into a courtyard in front of the kitchens. A small shed stood against the wall, and they squatted on the side farthest from the house. Chris peeked around the corner of the shed. To their left, a gate separated them from the garden itself. He could see where wagon wheels had worn grooves in the flagstones.

Like the ticking of a clock, drops of rain plip-plopped against the shed's roof.

"Ready?" he asked.

Terrin and Arnold nodded.

Chris started to rise, but froze as the door to the kitchens swung open. He ducked back quickly.

Anthony stepped out of the door, followed by Grith.

What are they, of all people, doing here? Chris slicked his damp hair out of his eyes, and wrapped his hand around his sword hilt. He saw Arnold's hand do the same.

Duke Grith spoke, his voice echoing in the courtyard. "Please, Christopher, come out so I can welcome you properly. I already know you're there." He chuckled. "Though I do commend your attempt at stealth."

Arnold leaned forward, but Chris blocked him.

"I honestly don't know why you're here," the duke continued, "but I'm pleased to have the chance to talk to you."

Chris heard the click of boots on the flagstones, walking towards them.

Wait for it, he mouthed.

❧

Arnold

Arnold's whole body vibrated with anticipation. He forced his grip on his sword hilt to relax, waiting until the duke drew near. Then he sprang forward, drawing his sword and swinging at the man with one motion.

"Wait," called Terrin, a second too late.

His sword hit thin air and bounced back, like it had struck a wall.

The duke flicked his wrist, and Arnold flew sideways.

"Arnold!" cried Terrin, running to stand between him and the duke, her knife drawn.

Anthony's sword slithered from its sheath.

"It's all right, Anthony. I have this under control," said Grith, taking a step back.

Looking closer, Arnold could see the rain splattering against empty air as it hit the edge of the duke's magic shield.

Chris rose from his hiding place, sword drawn. "Grith, I know what you're planning. You're a traitor to your country and your king."

"I doubt you know everything I'm planning. But I'd be interested in explaining it to you. If you calm down and put the sword away, that is. I really don't want to hurt you. You're part of my plan, you see."

"You did frame me for stealing the Shard, didn't you?"

"Yes, though that was Anthony's idea. It wasn't until later that I realized I needed you. But as I said, explanations can wait until you put away the sword."

Of course. Anthony wouldn't hesitate to frame his brother. The snake. Arnold drew himself onto one knee and adjusted his grip on his sword.

"Chris?" called Nora, running down the path. She stopped short at the sight of the duke and Anthony. She drew her own sword.

"Nora, get out of here," said Chris. He lunged at Grith.

The shield had disappeared, but the duke side-stepped, turning to grab Chris's arm as he passed by. "I told you to put your swords away. Children should listen to their elders. Perhaps this will convince you."

In one movement, Arnold jumped up and past Terrin, slashing at Grith.

Anthony stepped between them, catching Arnold's sword with his own blade and attempting to push him back. Arnold threw his weight forward against the swords, and instead it was Anthony who stumbled back.

Arnold grinned. *Take that, cousin.*

He pulled back his arm for another strike, but Anthony kicked his shin. Arnold's foot slipped on the wet pavement, and he fell. Grimacing, the older knight stepped away, as if waiting to see what Arnold would do next.

Not much of a knight, are you? Don't even know to press an advantage.

"Chris, stop," said Terrin.

As Arnold scrambled to his feet, he glanced her direction. And gasped. Chris's eyes had gone blank. He was striding towards Arnold, his sword raised.

"Chris," called Nora.

Chris paused for a second.

Terrin grabbed Arnold's arm and pulled him away. "Grith cast a spell on him," she said.

"So, forest people *can* sense magic. Interesting," said Grith.

"Now put away the swords, before you hurt each other."

Nora stepped forward. "Chris, fight it. You can beat him."

"Actually, he can't," said Grith. "You see, his resistance to magic is rather low. But since you won't shut up…"

Chris turned and started towards Nora.

"No," said Arnold, stepping between them.

Chris swung, but Arnold caught it with his own blade and, with a deft twist, sent Chris's sword flying. Chris took another step towards him. *Just like a mock duel,* Arnold told himself. He stepped forward and shoved his friend with the side of his arm so Chris stumbled and fell. But he bounced back up without so much as a blink. He swung a punch towards Arnold's face, and Arnold narrowly ducked.

It was nothing like a mock duel. Chris was fighting for real. What had Grith done to him?

Chris threw a second punch, just as Nora called, "Chris, stop!" His blow faltered.

Arnold braced himself for another shove at his friend, but he noticed movement in the corner of his eye. Anthony's sword striking out. He spun and deflected the blow so it only clipped his arm. Gritting his teeth, he stabbed at the traitor, who jumped back out of reach.

"Nora!"

At Terrin's cry, Arnold's focus slipped. Pain burned through his face as Anthony's sword cut his cheek. He knocked it away again and tried to put some space between him and his assailant, but the snake moved with him.

"I thought Uncle taught you better than this, Arnold. You're unfocused, and sloppy. How were you ever knighted, if you fight like this? Or is this the fault of your missing hand?"

Arnold lunged forward in a flurry of blows. "I'm still better than you," he snarled. The older knight had years of experience, but Arnold had learned from the best—his father.

"Arnold, help me," Terrin called. "I can't stop Chris alone."

Arnold darted sideways so he could see both Terrin and Anthony. He sucked in a deep breath. Chris had his hands wrapped around Nora's throat, and a bright red gash dripped down his back. Terrin had thrown her bloodied knife to the side and had one arm wrapped around his chest, trying to drag him back. Nora's face contorted with pain as she fought weakly.

It's his dream, from back in the mountains. I hadn't even thought of that.

"Stop fighting, Arnold. You can't win," said Grith.

At the duke's signal, Anthony stepped back, sword still raised.

Arnold hesitated.

What could he do? He might beat his cousin, but the duke— How could a knight fight against magic?

Then he saw Terrin's face. There were tears in her eyes. Tears that told him she felt just as helpless as he did.

His fist clenched, but Arnold lowered his sword and let it slide into his sheath. He bowed his head.

Even as he saw Anthony move, he felt a burst of pain at the back of his head.

❧ 35 ❧

Christopher

Pain. A burning pain along his back. The pain dragged Chris from his slumber and out into the real world.

"Ah, you're finally awake." Grith's voice brought Chris awake the rest of the way.

He sat up on the bed. A single flickering torch hung over a wooden table, illuminating the small room. Though the place looked clean, the stone wall stank of mildew.

Duke Grith sat in the single chair, his hands folded in his lap.

"Are you ready to talk, or do you want to throw a tantrum?" the duke asked.

"What happened? Where's Nora? And the others?" said Chris. He wanted to press himself into the corner, but that would make the throbbing pain worse.

"They're alive. Not so much healthy, but I've asked a healer to attend to them. You're the worst off. I imagine Terrin's given you a scar. She thought pain would snap you out of the trance, I suppose."

"And what about Trillory? She's in Charlon, isn't she?"

"Oh, so you know about your sister? Was that why you came rushing in, to say hello? Admittedly, she is my prisoner, but I have no intention of ever harming her. Her magical potential is too valuable. And I assure you, her accommodations are much nicer than yours."

She's not dead. That dream wasn't even about today.

"Then what is it you're so insistent on talking about?" said Chris, struggling to control his emotions.

Grith smiled—a predatory expression, with no hint of warmth. "As you have already guessed, I was responsible for stealing the Fredricburg Shard, and most of the other Shards, too. However, they are not in my possession. They all disappeared before I ever saw them. My guess is that they've returned to the cave where Miles first found the Stone. The cave the riddles are leading you to. Since you're the only one who can read the riddles, I need you to get them for me."

"Why do you need the Shards?"

"Despite what you think about me being the traitor, I have the best interest of the Raecs at heart. Both of them."

Chris rolled his eyes. *As if.*

The duke continued, "I have set in motion a plan to unite the countries once more. Unfortunately the Coric line has grown weak, so I am forced to take upon myself the burden of leading this fine country. Then I can use my power to put South Raec in its proper place as a subsidiary of the North. The Shards are a step to solidifying my claim to the throne."

"You have no claim to the throne."

Grith ran his hand over his black hair. "Not yet, but that's all part of the plan. Now, the Shards aren't entirely necessary, but they will make things simpler. Which is why I want you to fetch them. I was going to let you finish your quest on your own and get them from you later, but, since you're here, I think we can make a deal."

"Whether I find them or not, I will never give the Shards to you," Chris snarled.

"Even if the lives of your friends are in the balance? I will win either way, you know. Help me, and the four of you go free to live your lives in peace. Don't, and they'll die." The man laughed.

Chris bit his lip. His fingers dug into the rock-like mattress. "I will not betray my king."

Grith's smile vanished, and he sighed. "How about I give you some time to think about it? Discuss the situation with Terrin, I hear she's your adviser. She's in the next cell over. And Arnold's across the way. Nora's down the hall, where it'll be quieter. I would recommend you let her sleep."

༄

Terrin

The door slammed shut, and Terrin heard the click of Grith's boots fading away. She uncoiled her body from the chair and went to press herself against the stone wall.

"Chris?" she called.

"Terrin?" came his muffled voice. "Are you okay?"

"I'm in the best shape of all of us," she said wryly. "Sorry about your back. I was hoping that… since it got you out of the dream… I'm sorry."

"It's fine. Thanks for trying. I'm the one who's sorry. I should have known what was coming. Have you heard from Nora or Arnold?"

He spoke slowly, and she could imagine him leaning against

the wall for support, his eyes blank.

"No. Your brother hit Arnold pretty hard, so he might be out for a while. Nora… she'll be fine."

"How long do you suppose Thomas will wait for us?" he asked.

Terrin tried to swallow the lump that formed in her throat, but it bobbed back up.

Chris didn't know.

"He won't," she said.

❧

Nora

Nora barely noticed when she slipped into consciousness. One moment she was pulling the sheets tighter, the next she realized she shouldn't be in a bed.

She opened her eyes and immediately met the gaze of Thomas.

Frowning, she sat up and took in her surroundings. The rickety table and chair, the bed she sat on tucked into one corner, a simple wooden chest in the other. The chill air felt like sludge.

"Thomas, what are you—" she stopped and rubbed her throat. It felt tight, and the words caught and rasped.

"Don't talk, just drink this," he said, handing her a glass.

She took it and sipped, but her curiosity was too strong.

"How did Grith catch you?" she asked, whispering to ease the pain.

"It… I'm sorry Nora," Thomas said. His head bowed. His shoulder sagged. "I've been lying to you. I've been his agent all along."

"What?" Nora exclaimed, then winced.

"After my family died, the Healers' Guild was all I had left. When they banished me from their ranks… I didn't know what to do. Grith offered me the chance to become a healer again."

He hunched over, his willowy frame looking frailer than ever. Taking a deep breath, he continued.

"I thought all I had to do was research the riddles, but Grith tricked me. He cast a spell so if I disobey him, I'll die. I've been reporting to him all along. I'm sorry, I am, but I was weak."

Nora stared at him. Her chest felt hollow, but her body wouldn't move, wouldn't express emotion. She wanted to scream, and cry, and maybe punch him, but she couldn't.

"As long as Chris does what the duke wants, you'll all be safe," he said.

"Don't pretend you care," rasped Nora. "Don't act like you're still our friend."

Thomas flinched, and, despite herself, Nora felt bad.

She turned her face away.

She heard him walk to the door.

"Get some rest, Nora," he said. "You'll need it to heal."

"Wait," she said.

He stopped.

"Could… could you bring me my grandmother's bag? It's the small, painted, leather one?" She asked, blushing. "Surely something like that couldn't hurt?"

He smiled. "I'll see what I can do."

Nora drained the cup of liquid and set it to the side before curling herself into a ball.

☙

Arnold

Arnold crushed the flat pillow in his fist. His veins bubbled in rage as he listened to Chris and Terrin talking, but he couldn't bring himself to speak up. The hallway torches grew dim, leaving his room in shadow.

Thomas was my friend. I trusted him, he thought.

"Don't blame yourself, Terrin," said Chris. "There was never a reason to suspect him. And I invited him on the quest."

I was supposed to protect everyone, thought Arnold. *I couldn't even see what was right in front of me. Couldn't bring myself to recognize that it was his voice under that hood.*

"Maybe you're right," said Terrin. "But I'm supposed to be the skeptical one."

There was silence.

"Chris…" Terrin murmured. "What about Trill? Maybe if you tell the duke about Arnold's dream, he'll protect her. He said she was valuable to him, didn't he?"

"I don't think it matters what we do, Terrin. The dreams will come true. I knew for months that I would… that I would try to strangle someone. I knew about Grith's magic, I should have realized that this was where it would happen, but I charged in without thinking, without planning ahead…"

"Chris, that wasn't your fault. Even I didn't bother to think twice," exclaimed Terrin. "And you can't give up on Trill like that. She's your sister."

It was my fault, thought Arnold. *I brought us rushing in here on the chance we could change things. I wanted to save everybody, and saved no one.*

He squeezed his eyes shut, resisting the angry tears.

"Trill will die, the dream said so." The ice in Chris's voice froze Arnold's heart. "We can't stop it, but we can find a way out of here, find a way to defeat Grith and avenge her."

"How?" said Terrin.

"The magic has brought us this far. It will get us out of this. It's stronger than anything Grith has. We have to keep moving. Past mistakes can't be fixed, but that doesn't mean we should make new ones. And it doesn't mean we should stop trying."

❧

NOT THE END.

YET.

❧

ABOUT THE AUTHOR

Seventeen-year-old homeschooler Teresa Gaskins has a particular set of skills, many of which have no use in her day-to-day life. Her interests range from trapshooting, to lock picking, to playing the violin. But her greatest interest is storytelling, which she's been doing since before she could write.

Though she enjoys a variety of fiction, fantasy has always been Teresa's favorite genre. *Betrayed* is her third published book, and she hopes to keep writing as long as she has stories to tell.

Teresa lives in rural Illinois with her cat overlord Cimorene, her beloved pit bull Natasha, and the rest of her family.

If you would like to read more of her writing or send her a message, please visit her blog:

TeresaGaskins.com

Discover How the Adventure Began

Haunted by dreams.
On a quest for answers.

Christopher Fredrico liked the quiet life of a scholar-in-training. Plenty of spare time to spend with his friends. But the night Crown Prince Tyler came to dinner, everything changed.

Falsely accused of stealing a magical artifact and banished under threat of death, Chris leaves the only home he knows. But as he and his friends travel towards the coast, they find a riddle that may save a kingdom — or cost them their lives.

If you enjoy quest stories, check out *Banished* — the first episode in *The Riddled Stone,* a four-book serial fantasy adventure by homeschooled teen author Teresa Gaskins.

She tried to warn them.
They wouldn't listen.

As a child, Terrin of Xell barely escaped a spirit from the Dark Forest. She knows better than to rely on magic. But with her schoolmate Chris accused of a magical crime he didn't commit, she couldn't let him face banishment alone.

So Terrin gets caught up in Chris's quest to recover an ancient relic, with only magic to guide them.

Naturally, everything goes wrong.

What lurks in the shadows, hunting Terrin and her friends? Or did the magic itself turn against them?

Follow the rising stakes in *Hunted* — the second volume of Teresa Gaskins's four-book serial fantasy adventure *The Riddled Stone.*

...And What Comes Next

A gift she never wanted.
A curse she can't escape.

Alone in the dark, Nora of Yorc feels the dungeon walls pressing in. Even worse, the duke's sorcery weaves itself around her, unseen and deadly. But as the spell tightens, shy, fragile Nora breaks—and something new takes her place.

Or something old beyond memory.

Nora joined this quest to help her friends. But can she stop herself before the wildness within destroys them all?

If you love epic struggles of good against evil, don't miss *Revealed,* the exciting conclusion of Teresa Gaskins's four-book serial fantasy adventure, *The Riddled Stone.*

For ordering information visit:
TabletopAcademy.net/Fantasy-Fiction

Don't Miss Out!

Get Teresa's 50-page booklet of short stories and tips for young writers—and be one of the first to hear about her next book. Join the *Tabletop Academy Press Updates* email list on her blog or at the Tabletop Academy website:

TeresaGaskins.com
TabletopAcademy.net/Subscribe